W9-CFH-039

To Mrs. Thommen and Mrs. McAniff,
who first taught me to read and write.

# CHAPTER EIGHT

# Payback Time

Made a list of all persons we had harmed, and became willing to make amends to them all.

*—Step 8 of the Twelve Steps*

· · · · ·

"Nathan said to David, 'You are the man!'. . . And David said to Nathan, 'I have indeed sinned.'"

*—2 Samuel 12:7, 13*

· · · · ·

"In judging others, you condemn yourself, since you behave no differently than those you judge."

*—Romans 2:1*

· · · · ·

"If you are bringing your gift to the altar, and there remember that your brother or sister has anything against you, go first and be reconciled to him or her, and then come back and present your gift."

*—Matthew 5:23–24*

· · · · ·

# The Adventures of Pink Elephant Vol. 2

## The Land of a Million Elephants

Christine Amamiya

©2009 Esoterica, LLC
This novel is a work of fiction. Any references to historical events; to real people, living or dead; or to real locales are intended only to give the fiction a sense of reality and authenticity. Names, characters, places, and incidents either are the product of the author's imagination or are used fictiously, and their resemblance, if any, to real-life counterparts is entirely coincidental.

All rights reserved. Printed in the United States of America. No part of this book may be used or reproduced in any manner whatsoever without written permission except in the case of brief quotations embodied in critical articles and reviews. For information address inquiries to:

Rococo House
3145 E. Chandler Blvd. #110-128
Phoenix, Arizona 85048-8702
www.RococoHouse.com

Illustrations: Kazuo Miyagi and Christine Amamiya
Cover layout: Christine Amamiya
Interior layout: J. L. Saloff

Fonts: Adore, Garamond Premier Pro, Baskerville, Bickham Script, Worstaveld Sting

*First Edition*

Amamiya, Christine,
    The Adventures of Pink Elephant: Vol. 2

10-Digit ISBN: 0-9795332-1-X
13-Digit ISBN: 978-0-9795332-1-1
LCCN: 2009909203

Copyright information available upon request

*Printed on Acid Free Paper in the United States of America*

1.0

# *Table of Contents*

# The Land of
# a Million Elephants

# Into the Woods

"UGH," CHRISTIE SWEPT A TREE BRANCH OUT OF HER face with a hand sticky with sap. "How much longer do we need to walk for?" The branch sprung back, almost hitting Christie's younger sister Mandy in the face. Mandy ducked. The branch whacked Alyssa on the arm.

"Watch it!" Alyssa snapped, turning to see who was responsible.

"I'm sorry," Mandy said sincerely. Alyssa froze.

"Mandy! Uh, that's okay," she moved away quickly to join her friend Vanessa, and the two of them spent the rest of the trip whispering to each other and glancing in Mandy's direction.

"Hey, hurry up!" Christie turned around, looking grumpy. "Mandy, what's taking you so long?"

Mandy giggled. "I think Alyssa is still scared of me."

"*Still?*" Christie said, impressed. "Wow, that's a long time. Pink Elephant must have really scared them off last time."

Mandy looked depressed at the mention of Pink Elephant. The baby elephant had hatched in their pool last summer and caused them a lot of trouble, but they had soon grown to be the best of friends. The two sisters hid him from adults and snuck him food to eat, and Pink Elephant had helped them a lot too. He had accidentally scared the bullies that had bothered Mandy for so long. Plus, he had worked with Christie on a school project she thought she could never do. The sisters and their friends Peter and Marianne had tons of fun together with Pink Elephant until he had to leave Earth to help one of his friends, a twonk. Mandy was certain he would visit them any day now and spent a lot of time wondering what a twonk was and if she would ever get to meet one.

"Mandy? You there?" Christie waved a hand in front of Mandy's face.

"I'm fine," Mandy said, shaking her head. "Just a little sad about Pink Elephant. I really miss him."

"Sorry," Christie said, wiping mud off the side of her face with the back of her hand. "I didn't mean to get you down."

"It's okay," Mandy said. "Why do you hate the woods so much?"

"You just had to remind me," Christie growled. "Look at my hands. *This* is why I hate the woods." She lifted two hands covered with bug bites and spider webs. Mandy giggled.

The two of them were Wilderness Scouts, and their troop had to go into the woods and camp out during a long weekend. Christie was really good at selling cookies door-to-door (especially since she was so famous, thanks to Pink Elephant's help a couple of months ago), and she loved arts and crafts. But when it came to building campfires and pitching tents, Christie was always last in line to try.

"Aw, C'mon, Christie. It's not that bad. Marianne hates mosquitoes, and she's fine," Mandy said. "Plus, we *just* got out of the car like ten minutes ago!"

"I know," Christie sighed. Earlier in the morning they had

*Christie wiped mud off the side of her face with the back of her hand.*

driven up to the bottom of short trail, and they were hiking to the campsite nearby, carrying their tents and some snacks. "I guess I'm just a magnet for trouble."

"Christie! Mandy! Hurry up!" Marianne called from up ahead, ducking into some bushes.

Mandy and Christie followed her into a wide-open space, where Ms. Sawyers was standing with a clipboard, marking off names as the girls walked tiredly past her.

"Evans, Mandy, and Evans, Christie," Ms. Sawyers noted as Mandy dragged Christie by. "Okay, that's the last of you!" Ms. Sawyers tucked the clipboard under her arm and cupped her hands to her mouth. "Scouts! Listen up! Good job on the hike up here! Ms. Julian and I have set up poles with colored flags on them around the campfire, and I'm going to call out names and your color. Once you hear your color wait until I've finished reading everyone else's name before you go over to that flag. There are three people to each tent. Once you've met up with your teammates you can go ahead and start trying to set up your tent. Don't forget to read the instructions first, and if you have any questions, find Ms. Julian or me, okay? Be very careful. Any questions?"

There was a silence except for the whispering of leaves, and Mandy glanced over at Christie. "What if they won't let us be in the same group?"

"They will," Christie said, wiping her hands against the sides of a boulder. "Don't worry about it. Ew!" she coughed and waved her hands in the air. "Gnats, gro-oss!"

"Megan, you're team red. Casey, team green. Christie, blue. Mandy, blue—"

Mandy breathed a sigh of relief, then looked around for Marianne. Christie was busy scooting away from a spider.

"—Annie, green, Joy, green, Madison, red, and Marianne, blue."

"Yesss!" Christie crowed. "Okay, let's go."

The two made their way over to a bright blue flag. Marianne was already there, unzipping a duffle bag.

"I've got the tent," she said.

"Does anyone have bug spray?" Christie asked.

Mandy reached into her backpack and pulled out a spray can. "Close your eyes and your mouth," Mandy ordered. Christie scrunched her eyes shut and took a deep breath. Mandy covered her in bug spray just as Marianne opened her mouth to speak.

Marianne coughed. "Mandy, that's too much! Seriously guys, we gotta get started! Alyssa's almost done!"

Mandy looked over her shoulder and set the bug spray down. Sighing, she started to help Christie unpack the tent as Marianne opened the fold-up instructions.

"Okay. First we have to anchor the tent," Marianne began reading aloud. "'Unravel the tarp and spread on the ground.'"

"Where's the tarp?" Mandy asked.

"It should be in the bag," Marianne said, still looking at the diagram.

Christie frowned, searching. "Are you sure?"

"Yeah," Marianne looked up. "Hey!"

Christie and Mandy spun around. A few feet away the tarp lay perfectly flat on the ground.

"Whoa!" Christie said.

"That's creepy," Mandy said, staring.

"Uh, okay. Maybe one of the teachers helped us out when we weren't looking," Marianne looked back down at the sheet nervously. "'Next, install the crossbar,'" she paused and glanced up. So far, nothing else had changed. She looked back down at the instructions. "'Unroll the free-standing tent.' What does 'free-standing' mean?"

"I don't know," Mandy said, "but I guess we don't need to figure it out."

Marianne looked up again. The tent stood perfectly just a few feet away. "Oh my gosh! Okay, this is seriously weird."

"Maybe not that weird," Mandy said thoughtfully, pointing at her backpack. The other two girls turned to look. A lot of the food was gone.

"You don't think," Christie started, then stopped, a big grin spreading across her face.

"Let's go find out!" Mandy leapt to her feet excitedly, but Christie yanked her back down.

"Mandy!" Christie hissed. "You can't just leave now! Ms. Sawyers and Ms. Julian will freak out!"

"But I want to see him!"

"Me too, Mandy," Christie said. She wanted to run into the woods, but there were too many people around. They would get in huge trouble. "We're going to have to wait until night-time, when no one else is up."

Sighing, Mandy nodded. Marianne started reading again, this time a little louder, just in case *someone* was listening. "'Pull the waterproof, wind-breaking topper on.'"

There was a flutter and a whoosh, and the large green sheet was draped over the tent. Zippers whizzed around, fixing everything in place.

"Girls, team red and team green seem to have lost some of their food," Ms. Julian shouted. "If someone is stealing snacks and hogging it for themselves, please give it up now. We will not accept this kind of behavior."

Mandy, Christie, and Marianne looked at each other and burst out laughing.

"Girls! Something going on over there with team blue?" Ms. Julian called.

"Um, it's nothing! We're okay!" Mandy shouted. "Christie just lost control of the tent for a second."

"Hey!" Christie protested. Marianne giggled.

Ms. Julian and Ms. Sawyers walked by, looking worried.

"We've lost some of our own food, too, Betsy. What are we going to do? Do you think it could be some animal?" Ms. Sawyers was saying.

"I don't know," Ms. Julian sighed. "Maybe a badger or something. But we won't be able to make s'mores tonight."

"Do you think it's safe? What if it was a raccoon—they could be dangerous if they got angry!"

Ms. Julian frowned. "Dangerous?" she repeated.

"Pink elephants aren't," Mandy whispered under her breath, and the three girls held back their laughter as they unrolled their sleeping bags.

# Trail Trials

MANDY, CHRISTIE AND MARIANNE WAITED ALL NIGHT, but Ms. Julian and Ms. Sawyers were keeping a close watch on the camp, making sure that whoever was stealing the food wasn't coming back for more. The three girls had eventually drifted off to sleep, and woke with surprise the next morning to the sound of Ms. Julian's whistle.

"Why didn't Pink Elephant come see us?" Mandy frowned as they gathered around the campfire. "I *know* it was him, I just know it!"

"I know," Christie agreed. "It's so weird. I thought for sure he would sneak in to see us if we couldn't go see him."

"Maybe he's busy with something," Marianne said. "He might have a lot of stuff to do that we don't know about."

"Girls, come roast your hotdogs!" Ms. Sawyers walked by.

"Hot dogs for breakfast?" Mandy looked down at her sausage-on-a-stick.

"At least we *have* hotdogs," Christie pointed out through a mouthful of hotdog. "Pink Elephant might not have left us *any*."

"I still think it's kind of weird," Mandy said. "Didn't we teach him not to steal food without asking?"

"That's true," Christie frowned. "It *does* seem kind of impolite of him. Plus he would never take food from us if he thought we were hungry."

"But no one else could steal that much food that fast!" Marianne pointed out. "If Pink Elephant isn't taking the food, who is?"

The three girls fell silent, wondering.

"Attention, girls!" Ms. Julian's voice rang out. "Today we will be doing our annual scavenger hunt. Each team will be the same team that shared a tent. Ms. Sawyers is passing out sheets of paper and a couple of plastic bags. The sheet of paper will have a map on the back telling you where to go, and on the front will be a list of three things you will be asked to find and bring back to us. The first team to get back to the campsite with all three items will be the winning team. Don't forget to use your compasses, like we learned yesterday. If there's an emergency, you will stay where you are and blow on the silver whistles we will give you at the starting line. We will be close behind you. *Do not go off any trails*. Any questions?"

There was an excited murmur and Marianne turned to Christie with raised eyebrows. "Are you thinking what I'm thinking?" she asked.

"Yeah. We can look for Pink Elephant on the way. He'll probably find us first, though," Christie mumbled, her mouth still full.

Mrs. Sawyers reached their group and handed them a large sheet of paper. "You guys are team blue, right?"

Mandy nodded.

"This is the trail you will be following," Mrs. Sawyers said, pointing out a thin blue line drawn on the map. She flipped the map over. "You are asked to collect one wild berry, two kinds of moss, and an acorn. Good luck!"

Marianne finished her hot dog and tossed the stick back into the fire. "Guess we'd better go over there," she said, nodding at the large red start line that had been spray-painted onto the ground.

The three girls trudged over to the line, where Mrs. Julian hung a whistle around each of their necks.

"Hey guys," Alyssa said to them with a grin. "Think you'll win the hunt?"

Mandy shrugged, looking suspiciously at Vanessa, who was sneaking up behind them. "Maybe. Do you?"

Alyssa giggled. "You've got to be kidding me. I'm terrible with the outdoors. What do you guys have to find?"

Mandy opened her mouth to speak, but Christie beat her to it. "It's none of your business. Go get with the rest of your group and leave her alone."

Alyssa made a sour face. "Fine. C'mon, Vanessa." The two skipped off, grinning and looking over their shoulders at Mandy.

"Christie, she was actually being nice to me," Mandy groaned. "Why did you have to chase them off?"

"That was pretty tough," Marianne agreed, crossing her arms.

Christie glared at the two of them. "I don't think she was just trying to be friends. Something's fishy about this. Mandy, zip up your backpack! You gotta be ready!"

"What?" Mandy slipped her backpack off her shoulders and zipped it back up. "I thought I did already!"

Christie frowned, looking around suspiciously.

"Alright, everyone's ready!" Mrs. Sawyer's voice boomed. "Remember, even if you haven't got all your stuff, please be back at the campsite by noon, because that's when we're going to end the hunt. When I blow my whistle you guys are off! One, two, and three!"

There was a sharp, piercing whistle and everyone dashed

off into the woods. Mandy looked down at the map as they jogged. "We have to climb over a large boulder shaped like a rabbit," she said.

"I see it!" Marianne said, pointing up ahead. "C'mon!"

The three of them put on an extra burst of speed, and ten minutes later were climbing up the sides of "the rabbit".

"It *does* look like a rabbit," Mandy said excitedly. "Look, there are even two parts that look like ears."

"Moss usually grows on rocks," Marianne said, looking at the boulder carefully. "Maybe we can pick up one of our items already."

"I found some!" Christie exclaimed. "There's only one type, though."

"Lemme see!" Mandy crawled over to where the rock began to dip down into the rabbit's back. "Can you scrape it off?"

Christie rubbed her thumbnail against it and a little fell into the plastic bag Marianne held underneath.

"One down, two more to go," Mandy said happily, looking into the bag.

"Three more," Marianne corrected. "We have to find another kind of moss. And finding the berries might be hard. It's too early in the year."

"Well, we might find some wild strawberries," Christie said.

"It's already March; there might be some early ones. Anyway, where do we go next? What does the map say?"

Mandy looked. "Go north for about a hundred feet," she said. "Which way is north?"

"Get out your compass and see," Marianne said, covering her eyes from the sun with a hand. It was getting warmer already. Christie looked down at her watch. It was ten-fifteen.

"I can't find it!" Mandy shouted a moment later. She patted down her pockets frantically. "I don't have my compass!"

"What!?" Marianne zipped open Mandy's backpack and dug through the stuff inside. "Christie, do you have yours?"

"I left mine in the tent," Christie gasped. "I thought since Mandy was bringing hers I wouldn't need mine!"

"Oh no!" Marianne wailed. "I lost mine yesterday on the hike!"

"Okay, try not to panic," Christie said. "Maybe we can find our way back to the campsite and get mine from the tent. We haven't gone that far yet."

"I don't get it!" Mandy kept searching. "I *know* I put it in here this morning!"

Marianne froze. "*Vanessa!*"

"What?"

"It was Vanessa! Remember they came over to talk to us–"

"And my backpack was unzipped afterwards!" Mandy shouted. "She took my compass!"

Marianne was furious. "I can't *believe* that girl."

"Okay. We have got to stay calm," Christie said. "We can still go back."

Mandy could hear her heart pounding in her chest as she looked over at the stretch of forest. "I don't know, Christie. Mrs. Sawyers said that if anything happened we should stay where we are." She lifted her whistle to her lips.

"Wait!" Christie yanked Mandy's whistle away.

"Christie, what are you doing!?"

"Listen. We just started. If we need help already, everyone's going to think we can't do anything on our own!"

"But Christie, here for sure they'll be able to hear us and find us! Isn't it more important that we get saved?"

"We're not Wilderness Scouts for nothing," Christie protested. "We'll just go back ourselves. Besides, remember, Pink Elephant is in here somewhere. He'll be able to find us and help us if we're in trouble."

Mandy fell silent at the mention of Pink Elephant.

"Marianne, what do you think?" Christie looked at Marianne.

"I guess...if Pink Elephant's here, we'll be okay."

Mandy sighed. "Fine. We'll go back."

The three of them scrambled down the rock and into the woods.

Half an hour later the girls were still struggling through bushes and over large rocks. They were completely, utterly lost.

"I gotta rest," Christie said, sitting down on a tree stump.

"This is all your fault," Marianne said angrily. "If you care so much about your reputation, you should have just gone back without us!"

"We can't be *that* lost," Christie argued.

"We *are!*" Mandy stomped her foot. "I am going to blow this whistle and nobody is going to stop me!" she put it to her lips and blew with all her might. Some birds in a nearby tree squawked and flapped away. Then there was silence.

Marianne tried her own whistle, and then both Mandy and Marianne blew until they felt dizzy. There was no answer.

"Just great," Mandy said. "Now we're really lost and nobody can find us!"

Suddenly, there was a low rumble. The girls could hear trees crashing somewhere in the forest.

"What was that?" Mandy whispered, eyes wide. Marianne and Christie stared back at her.

The rumbling noise was getting bigger and bigger, and they saw the tops of some trees sway and fall, thundering, out of sight.

"What if it's a bear?" Marianne screamed in a whisper.

There was a large, dark shape moving clumsily through the trees. Mandy squeezed her eyes shut and hugged Christie tightly. There was another silence.

"Um...um...haloooooo. Um...are you, um, loooooooost?"

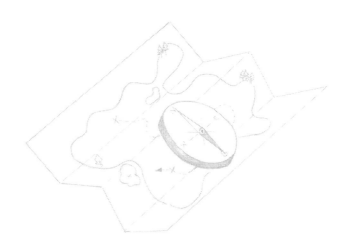

# A Rather Large Problem

THE THREE GIRLS SCREAMED AT THE TOP OF THEIR lungs. A huge man stood in front of them, over six feet tall. His hair was thick, dark gold and a little curly, and his eyes were a bright blue. The strange thing was that he walked as though he weighed thousands of pounds, even though the girls were pretty sure that no one weighed that much. He was probably thirty years old.

He was wearing a white T-shirt with a logo the size of Mandy's palm on his right sleeve. It showed a large golden scale with two hanging baskets that formed the letter 'T'. A huge man held one of the baskets on one side, while an elephant held up the other basket. Both baskets were filled with food. The man holding the basket was

wearing a thick, black, strange-looking belt around his waist, and Mandy realized with a jolt that the man in front of them was wearing the same belt.

"Wait a minute," Marianne said, pointing at the logo. "Is that a *pink*—"

"Twonkie-Twonkie!" a familiar voice shouted. "You're not supposed to scare other people!"

Something small and pink came whizzing out from the bushes. Mandy felt excitement run through her, washing her tiredness away. She *hoped* it was *him!*

"PINK ELEPHANT!"

"Hello!" Pink Elephant flew towards Mandy, who gave him a big hug. He was in his stuffed-animal size, the size of a teddy bear, and fit into her arms perfectly.

"We missed you!" Marianne and Christie crowded around Mandy.

"When did you get here?"

Christie hugged him tightly. "I'm so, so glad to see you again."

"Me too!" Pink Elephant tapped each of their noses with his trunk, smiling.

"Why didn't you come see us, Pink Elephant?" Mandy asked. "We waited all night!"

"I'm sorry," Pink Elephant's ears drooped. "I really wanted

to come see you too! But I had to keep Twonkie-Twonkie company. I *did* help set up your tent, though."

"I *knew* it was you!" Mandy said.

"What happened in Twonkie Land?" Christie asked excitedly. "Tell us about your adventures!"

"Well," Pink Elephant said cheerfully, "first I have someone to introduce to you. Everyone, please meet Twonkie-Twonkie, my dear friend. Sometimes people just call him 'Twonkie.'"

"*That's* a twonk?" Christie exclaimed, her jaw dropping.

"Christie!" Mandy hissed. "Be polite!"

"But he looks just like a normal guy!" Christie said. "Well, except..."

"He's kinda big," Marianne whispered.

"Guys!" Mandy sighed. "I'm sorry, Twonkie-Twonkie. My friends are being rude. My name is Mandy."

"Um, um, nice to, um, meeeet you," Twonkie-Twonkie said.

"I'm Christie, Mandy's sister," Christie said.

"Hallooo."

"And I'm Marianne! I have a little brother named Peter, but he's not here right now," Marianne turned to Pink Elephant. "Peter can meet Twonkie later, right?"

"Of course!" Pink Elephant smiled.

"You seem very, um, um, niiiice," Twonkie-Twonkie said.

"What are you doing here on Earth?" Mandy asked.

Twonkie brightened. "Twonkie is taking, um, Earth, um, Studies. Twonkie must, um, study living creatures, um, on Earth. It is, um, a very special program. Um, only, um, one Twonkie has ever done it before."

"Who?" Marianne wanted to know.

"Um, the Great Twinkie-Twinkie of the North. Um, he even, um, tried to meet with humans, but they, um were scared of him. They, um, called him, um," Twonkie scratched his head. "Twonkie cannot remember. Um, Twonkie thinks he was called, um, 'Big Arm.'"

"Big Foot!" Christie exclaimed.

"The Great Twinkie-Twinkie of the North was so heavy that a lot of things used to get broken around him," Pink Elephant explained. "He even caused some stars to explode by accident."

"*Explode!?*" Marianne said. "Like, blow up?"

"Yes," Pink Elephant nodded. "There used to be a song about him. It went,

> *Twinkie-Twinkie's little star,*
> *how I wonder where you are.*
> *Are you in the sky, still here?*
> *Did Twinkie make you disappear?*"

*Twinkie-Twinkie's little star, how I wonder where you are.*

"Wait," Mandy said. "Didn't it actually go, 'Twinkle, Twinkle, little star, how I wonder what you are. Up above the sky so high, like a diamond in the sky'?"

"The words got a little lost after a while," Pink Elephant said. "It happens sometimes."

"Oh," Mandy said.

"I can't believe it!" Marianne said excitedly. "Almost everything we know is related to pink elephants and twonks!"

"Because, um, humans, um, um, did not like the Great

Twinkie-Twinkie of the North, ummm, all future, um, Earth Studies were stopped," Twonkie-Twonkie went on. "But, um, because Twonkie's, um, good friend Pinky came to um, Earth, um, he told Twonkie's um, teachers that, um, um, he would watch over Twonkie."

"Who's 'Pinky'?" Marianne cocked her head.

"That's my nickname," Pink Elephant explained.

"What are you studying on Earth?" Mandy asked.

"Um, um, Twonkie is supposed to, um, look at, um, small creatures. Um, Twonkie tried to look at, um, a biiiird, but, um, he could only find this, um, squash."

Twonkie dug into his pocket, then held out his hand. In it was a squirrel, trembling nervously. Twonkie made soft shushing noises, and surprisingly, the squirrel calmed down.

"Twonks are, um, very good with, um, animals," Twonkie explained, as Mandy, Christie, and Marianne looked on in awe. "They can, um, kind of, um, um, talk to them."

"Cool!"

"This squash, um, actually, um, told Twonkie-Twonkie that there was good food nearby," Twonkie said.

"Wait a minute!" Mandy said, laughing. "Did *you* steal all the food from the Wilderness Scouts?"

"Um, um, yes," Twonkie-Twonkie said. He hung his head. "Twonkie is, um, sorry."

*Twonks are very good with animals.*

Pink Elephant sighed.

Mandy laughed. "You like to eat food a lot, huh? Just like Pink Elephant."

"It is why we are such good friends," Pink Elephant smiled. "Twonks might not move very fast in general, but there is a saying in pinkelephantian, 'faster than a shooting star or a Twonk looking for food.' They move so fast when there's food that humans can barely see them."

"Whoa!" Christie said. "What do you eat, Twonkie-Twonkie?"

"Um, um, everything," Twonkie said.

"He really means everything," Pink Elephant said.

"Rocks, um, um, are Twonkie's, um, faaavorite."

"*Rocks!?*" the three girls said. They were pretty sure even Pink Elephant didn't eat those.

"Twonkie's favorite are, um, um, the crunchy ones."

Mandy and Christie gave each other a look. What kind of rocks weren't crunchy?

"Any good rocks around here?" Christie wanted to know.

"Um, most are, um, um, not that crunchy," Twonkie-Twonkie frowned, thinking hard. "Except for one, um, very um, sparkling one."

"That was a diamond," Pink Elephant said.

"A *diamond!?*" all three girls exclaimed.

"No way!" Christie said. "You ate a *diamond?*"

"Well, diamonds *are* the hardest thing ever in nature," Mandy said knowledgeably.

"Also, even though, um, um, it was not crunchy, um, Twonkie found one that tasted good. It um, looked like, um, a rabbun."

"He means a rabbit," Pink Elephant said.

"A rabbit?" Marianne was puzzled.

"No *wonder* we couldn't find our way back!" Christie said. "Remember after we got lost the first time we wanted to go back to the rabbit rock, and we couldn't find it!"

"Oh my gosh!" Mandy said. "But...but...that rock was huge!" There was no way one person could have eaten the whole thing. But then again, Twonkie-Twonkie clearly wasn't a regular person.

"Twonkie is, um, sooorrry," Twonkie said again.

"Don't worry about it," Christie said. "We're okay now. We can just stay with you."

Twonkie looked pleased.

"But Christie," Marianne said, glancing down at her watch, "it's almost eleven. What if the other teams have already gotten their stuff and gone back to the camp? And we need to be back by twelve!"

"Twonkie, do you think you could find our camp?" Mandy asked.

Twonkie shook his head. "Twonkie is, um, very bad with, um, directions. The only time, um, um, he could find you was, um, because you made the sharp noise."

"He's talking about your whistles," Pink Elephant explained.

"Yes," Twonkie-Twonkie nodded. "It made, um, um, the squash very nervous."

"It's a squirrel, Twonkie," Christie said gently.

"Um, um, scu-arral."

"Close enough," Marianne grinned.

"Why did you use your whistles?" Pink Elephant asked. "Were you lost?"

"Yes, we were," Mandy said. "We would have used our compasses, but I couldn't find mine and Christie left hers in the tent and Marianne had already lost hers yesterday!"

"We think Vanessa took Mandy's," Marianne explained.

Pink Elephant frowned even more. "I just remembered. As I was flying over the forest I heard her say you and Christie and Marianne would be lost for sure without your compass. That's why I came to find you!"

"Thanks, Pink Elephant," Mandy said, hugging him again. "You're the best."

"Don't worry," Pink Elephant said. "There is still time to fix the problem. I can bring you back!"

"But we have to get other stuff!" Mandy said. "We can't go back until we finish the scavenger hunt. We still need a wild berry, another kind of moss, and an acorn."

"Hmm," Pink Elephant closed his eyes and concentrated. "I remember seeing a small patch of wild strawberries, and I know where there is another spot on a tree for moss!"

"Wow!" Christie was in awe. "You can remember everything you saw exactly?"

"Yes!" Pink Elephant said, curling his trunk up. His ears drooped suddenly. "But I can't remember any acorns."

"Um, Twonkie knows!" Twonkie-Twonkie said. "Um, um, Scuarral can find the acorn."

"Really?" Mandy said.

Twonkie-Twonkie nodded and looked down at the squirrel. "Scuarral, um, um, you must find, um, good acorns, um, for Twonkie's friends," Twonkie lowered the squirrel to the floor. It stood there quivering for a moment, and then dashed off into some bushes. Meanwhile, Pink Elephant was looking at Mandy's map and pointing out where the strawberries and moss were.

"But how will we get there?"

Pink Elephant grinned. "You can fly on my back!"

Everyone stared in shock.

"Did you just say—*fly?*" Mandy whispered.

"Like, fly for real?" Marianne said in awe. "Could we really do that?"

"Yes!" Pink Elephant started growing bigger, until he was the size of a small car. "I promise it is safe! I will take care of you."

"Let's do it!" Mandy squealed, grabbing Christie's hand tightly. "This is going to be *so* cool!"

"Oh my gosh!" Marianne started screaming in excitement, jumping up and down. "I can't *believe* this!"

"Let's go!" Mandy started to climb up onto Pink Elephant's

back. He helped her by boosting her with his trunk, and Christie followed quickly.

"Come on, Marianne!" both sisters shouted.

Marianne pulled herself onto Pink Elephant's back, and then he started to hover over the floor. Christie started to shake a little bit, and Marianne grabbed onto Christie's waist, squeezing her eyes shut.

"Here we go!" Pink Elephant trumpeted loudly, and then they were darting up into the clouds.

# Speak Softly and Carry a Pink Elephant

"THIS IS SO COOL!" MANDY SHOUTED OVER THE ROAR OF the wind. "Open your eyes, Marianne!"

"I'm scared of heights!" Marianne shouted back, eyes squeezed shut. She cracked open one eye and peeked down at the forest beneath them. She could see Twonkie-Twonkie growing smaller and smaller, waving until he was out of sight.

"We can't see anything that far down," Christie yelled. "How can you know where we are?"

"Just a feeling," Pink Elephant said cheerfully, and then they were swooping through the clouds again, up and down, faster and faster, like they were on a crazy rollercoaster.

"All the blood is rushing to my head!" Christie screamed as Pink Elephant went into a dive. Just when Christie thought they couldn't go any faster, they were suddenly soaring upwards once more.

*Woo-hooo! This is so awesome!*

"AHHHHHHHHHHHHHHHH!" Marianne closed her eyes and grabbed Christie tightly.

Mandy raised her hands up in the air. "Woo-hooo! This is so awesome! Raise your hands, guys! It's more fun!"

"I can't raise my arms," Marianne yelled, "because I'm HOLDING ON FOR DEAR LIFE!"

They dropped down with a whoosh and a thump, and Marianne opened her eyes slowly. Just as Pink Elephant had promised, they were in the middle of a patch of wild strawberries.

"Here we are!" Pink Elephant threw out his trunk in front of him like a giant vacuum cleaner, and then with a great gushing noise several hundred strawberries flew straight into his mouth. He chewed and swallowed. "These are really good! A little sour, though. They're not completely ripe yet."

"Pink Elephant!" Christie exclaimed. "You ate all of them!"

"Nope," Pink Elephant shook his head. "There are some right there!" He pointed at their feet.

The girls looked down. Sure enough, there was a small cluster of strawberries just beside Mandy's sneakers.

Marianne stared. "Did you know how to do that before?"

"Nope!" Pink Elephant said, smiling contentedly. "It's just a little trick I picked up."

Mandy bent down and scooped the strawberries into another bag. "Now all we need are the moss and the acorns!"

Marianne checked her watch. "It already past eleven," she said. "We have to hurry!"

The three girls scrambled onto Pink Elephant's back, holding on tightly.

"It's going to take a while to get used to this," Christie said as they floated around a large mountain. "Where are we going now?"

"Somewhere in Nebraska," Pink Elephant said, speeding up. Mandy closed her eyes and let the wind rush through her hair.

"But Pink Elephant, we have to get stuff from the same forest we were in!" Marianne reminded him.

Pink Elephant's ears drooped slightly in discouragement, then flicked back up again. "No problem!" he said, turning hard to the right. The ground below them passed in a blur of color, streets and roads snaking through, rivers bursting wide and narrowing again. By the time Pink Elephant slowed down, green fields stretched for miles beneath them. The fields soon shrank into the distance as Pink Elephant landed again in a grove of trees covered in moss.

Without even climbing down from Pink Elephant's back, Marianne leaned over and scraped at some moss-covered bark, collecting it in a bag. She had hardly sealed the plastic zipper before Pink Elephant took off again.

"Slow down!" Marianne shouted. Mandy and Christie just grinned.

Squinting through the wind, the girls could see familiar woods rushing under them. Up ahead, a tall figure standing in the middle of the clearing.

"Hi!" Mandy called, waving hard. "Twonkie-Twonkie, we're back!"

The four of them landed with a *whump!*

"Um, that was, um, um, very fast," Twonkie-Twonkie said, smiling. Christie checked her watch. It had been about ten minutes since they had left.

"Wow!"

The Squirrel spit out the acrons and offered them to Mandy.

"Did the squirrel bring back the acorn?" Mandy asked anxiously. Before she could finish her sentence, there was a rustle of leaves and the squirrel exploded out of a nearby bush with an acorn stuffed in each of its cheeks. It had been running very fast, and its tail was a huge fluffy thing that made it look like there was a second squirrel attached to the first one. It was out of breath. Mandy bent down to see it better and it froze.

"Um, um, these are, um, Twonkie's friends," Twonkie told the squirrel. "They are, um, nice people."

The squirrel spat out the acorns and offered them to Mandy.

"Thank you!" Mandy said, beaming. Behind her Marianne and Christie watched with raised eyebrows. They had never seen such a crazy thing before.

Mandy put the acorns in the last bag and made sure she had everything in her backpack. The squirrel climbed up Twonkie-Twonkie's leg and disappeared into his pocket.

"Ready to go back?" Pink Elephant asked excitedly. "I bet we can still win!"

"Yeah!" Mandy climbed onto his back, followed by Marianne and Christie. This time Pink Elephant kept low, close to the treetops. After a while he sunk down, until they were behind a row of bushes. They could see through the branches straight into the camp, where Mrs. Sawyers and Mrs. Julian were waiting by the red finish line.

"We *are* first!" Pink Elephant grinned, shrinking into his usual stuffed-animal, teddy-bear size and climbing into Mandy's backpack. He zipped himself in with his head poking out so he could see what was going on.

"Ready, guys?" Mandy looked at Marianne and Christie.

"Ready!"

Taking a deep breath, the three of them walked out and crossed the line together.

"You guys are the winners!" Mrs. Sawyers cheered.

"I found two compasses in your tent, girls," Mrs. Julian said, handing out water bottles. "And I know Marianne lost hers yesterday. How did you ever manage to find your way around without it?"

"Oh," Marianne said, "we just...followed the position of the sun."

"That's right," Christie said. "You know...the position of the sun and the angle it makes with the ground...that kind of stuff."

"You know," Mrs. Sawyers said, "I think I remember reading an article in the newspaper a couple months ago about you doing some kind of community service for your school that had to do with the stars?"

Pink Elephant twitched in the backpack with silent laughter, and Mandy had to turn to block him from sight.

"Um, yeah," Christie mumbled, "that was me."

"You girls must be so good at astronomy and math!" Mrs. Julian said, impressed. "When you graduate from the Gold level you'll make great Wilderness Scout leaders."

"Really?" Marianne grinned at Mandy and Christie.

"Let's just make sure you have everything," Mrs. Julian said, and Mandy reached into her backpack and pulled out the four plastic bags.

"I was a little worried about sending all you girls out there," Mrs. Sawyers said as Mrs. Julian took a look at the wild strawberries. "At one point we thought we heard an elephant!"

"But there's no way an elephant could be in the forest here," Mandy said, laughing nervously. "Right?"

"Of course not, dear," Mrs. Sawyers comforted Mandy. "It was probably just our imagination."

There was a shout behind them, and everyone turned just in time to see Alyssa, Vanessa, and another curly-haired girl cross the finish line.

Alyssa's mouth curved into a wicked smile. "Been here all day, girls? Didn't get very far before Mrs. Sawyers and Mrs. Julian had to save you?"

"Actually," Mandy said, "you guys take second-place. Congratulations!"

"But...but how?" Alyssa said, staring in shock. She turned to look at Mandy, and it was then that she noticed Pink Elephant's head sticking out.

"AHHHH!!" She screamed. "It's that...that...you brought..." The words died on her lips.

Mandy looked over her shoulder. "What, this? Oh yeah, you remember I used to bring it with me to class in second grade. Um, sometimes it's nice just to have it around."

Alyssa stared in horror. Pink Elephant just winked.

# A Little Rock Music

THE REST OF THE WEEKEND CAMP-OUT PASSED QUICKLY. The three girls were in high spirits. Alyssa, desperate for a last attempt to get back at Mandy, had tried to sneak a jar of spiders into her tent in the middle of the night. Pink Elephant had been out with Twonkie-Twonkie, stargazing and talking with some night owls. When they came back, they were shocked to find the tent crawling with bugs. Fortunately, pink elephants do not have issues with spiders.

Early in the morning, Mandy woke up and stared at the spiders lined up neatly in front of the tent flap.

"W-what's going on?" she asked Pink Elephant.

"Twonkie-Twonkie and I found a lot of spiders in your tent last night," Pink Elephant explained. "He asked them not to bother you guys but they said it was really cold outside, so he told them they could stay in here until it gets warmer as long as they stay away from you."

*The spiders lined up neatly in front of the tent flap.*

Sure enough, as the sun rose, the spiders formed two lines and exited the tent in neat rows. Mandy woke Marianne and Christie up to watch.

"Twonkie-Twonkie told them they should be polite all the time," Pink Elephant said, yawning and curling up next to Mandy. "But spiders are usually polite. Don't worry."

The girls were woken again a few minutes later by screaming. They stumbled outside just in time to see Alyssa claw her way out of her tent, shrieking at the top of her lungs. They later learned from Twonkie that a couple of the most polite spiders had gone to find Alyssa to thank her for letting them stay in Mandy's tent. Christie laughed so hard she cried.

Before they knew it, it was time to go back home. Pink Elephant had to stay with Twonkie-Twonkie, who had never been to a human city before, and wanted to stay in the woods.

"I'll visit soon," Pink Elephant promised. "And I'll bring you back to visit Twonkie-Twonkie."

Just one day after they had gotten home, Mandy was climbing into bed when there was a light tap at the window. She slid the window open and Pink Elephant flew in, beaming. This time, he was the size of a keychain. Mandy smiled.

"Hello! Do you want to see something amazing?" Pink Elephant asked.

"What is it?" Christie came in from the bathroom, where she had been getting ready for bed.

"Twonks have more than just the ability to talk to animals," Pink Elephant said. "I want to show you another one of Twonkie-Twonkie's gifts."

"Okay!" Mandy said. "Let's go!"

"Wait!" Christie held up a hand. "Mom will come in to check on us and find out we're not here! And we can't be gone all night; we have school tomorrow!"

Mandy rolled her eyes. "C'mon Christie, don't be such a grownup."

"I promise to bring you back quickly," Pink Elephant said.

"Well, okay," Christie said. "But I don't want Mom to worry."

They heard footsteps on the stairs and quickly climbed into bed. Pink Elephant hid under Mandy's comforter. They lay there for a few minutes, until the door swung softly open.

"G'night Mom," Mandy mumbled.

"Goodnight girls," Mrs. Evans said. "Sweet dreams."

She closed the door. Instantly Mandy was out of bed.

"Okay! Let's get going!" she whispered, pulling on a jacket.

The two girls crept towards the window and climbed out onto Pink Elephant's back. Pink Elephant checked once to

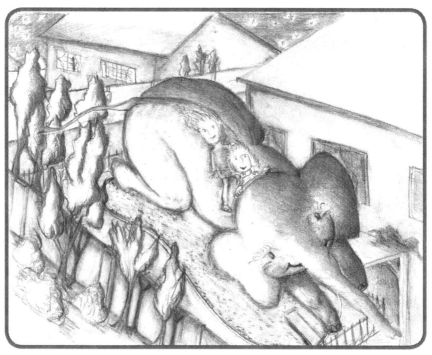

They took off into the sky.

make sure no one was looking out their windows, then took off into the sky. The night was cool and inky around them.

"The stars are so pretty," Mandy marveled.

"It is so interesting to see how they look like from Earth," Pink Elephant said. "They look completely different from Pinky Land."

In a few minutes, they had landed in the same campsite their Wilderness Scout Troop had used. It looked kind of lonely in the moonlight, empty except for the piles of ashes from burnt-out campfires.

"This way," Pink Elephant said, leading them into the forest.

"What's that?" Mandy asked. A soft, beautiful melody was coming through the trees. Someone was singing. The low notes seemed to hang in the air, while suddenly above them higher notes drifted and swelled like soft waves.

Christie shivered. The music was so gorgeous she was getting goosebumps. "Who would be here in the middle of the night?"

"Shhh," Pink Elephant said. "It's Twonkie-Twonkie." He parted the bushes in front of them and they peeked out.

"Oh my gosh," Mandy breathed.

In the middle of a small, rocky clearing, Twonkie-Twonkie stood in the moonlight. His eyes were closed and he was rocking back and forth on his feet very gently. His mouth was open in song.

"Wow," Christie whispered.

Around them small night birds and animals gathered. Mandy was a little nervous at first, but relaxed when she saw how tame they were. They were drawn to the music, focused on nothing else.

There was a deep rumbling, something even lower than Twonkie's voice. It sounded like the Earth was singing back, so low Mandy and Christie could barely hear it. The rocks around Twonkie's feet shivered and shimmered slightly, as though the girls were looking at them through a heat wave. The rumbling got louder, and the rocks began to bead up into small, perfectly round balls, each one the size of a fingernail.

"What's going on?" Mandy whispered to Pink Elephant.

"Just watch," Pink Elephant whispered back.

The boulders around Twonkie-Twonkie started to shimmer, too, until suddenly the music changed into a stronger melody and the rocks began to lengthen and narrow, spinning slowly upwards like upside-down tornadoes. Mandy and Christie grabbed each other. The tops of the tornadoes melted down into themselves as easily as if they had been made of clay, spreading out and forming into arches and flowery spreads. The small, perfectly round beads rolled up the sides of the tornado shapes, which were already thickening and widening. They sunk themselves into the larger rock, forming decorations over the archways already in place. The music was getting more and more complicated, with trills and more complicated rhythms chiming in.

Suddenly Mandy understood. "It's a castle," she whispered to Christie excitedly. "Oh my gosh, it's a castle, Christie. Look!"

And indeed it did look like a castle, like the Antonio Gaudí masterpiece *Sagrada Família* Christie had read about in class.

"How—how does he do that?" Christie gaped.

"There's more than one voice, too," Mandy turned to Pink Elephant. "How can one person sing with more than one voice?"

"Shhh," Christie said. "It's changing!"

The music was getting softer, slowing down, and the other voices in the song were dying away until there was only the main melody, still strong. The boulders groaned and the castle sunk down until, with the last notes of the song, they turned back into the regular rocks they had been before.

Mandy and Christie sat stunned in the silence. It seemed that not a living thing in the whole forest was stirring. For just a moment, Mandy had believed the Earth had added its voice to Twonkie's song, that the trees had been the soft chorus humming along, and that the stars overhead had been the light

dancing notes at the highest part of the music. And now it felt like a fantastic dream, except that her body was filled with happiness and love, and she knew that she would never hear music more beautiful than Twonkie's in her entire life.

# An Elephant in Need Is Pink Elephant Indeed

THE NEXT MORNING MANDY AND CHRISTIE WENT TO school still in a trance. Marianne met them at the bus stop, Peter in tow.

"Hey guys!" Peter said.

Marianne waved her hand in front of Mandy's face. "Guys? What happened?"

"We heard the most *gorgeous* music last night," Christie sighed.

"What do you mean?"

The bus arrived and the four friends got on. Mandy explained how Pink Elephant had taken them to listen to Twonkie-Twonkie's singing.

"I had the best dreams, afterwards," Mandy said.

"Me too," Christie agreed. "I felt so happy and relaxed."

"Man," Marianne sighed. "All the best stuff happens when we're not there."

"Yeah," Peter said. "Can you guys come get us next time?"

"I'll ask Pink Elephant later," Christie said as the bus pulled up to the school. "I don't see why not!"

In class Mrs. Wilson, Marianne and Christie's fifth-grade teacher, announced there would be another project, due in a few weeks.

"Great," Christie groaned to Marianne. "*Another* project."

"What happened to regular, normal homework?" Marianne agreed.

"We're going to learn about endangered animals," Mrs. Wilson went on. "Two students to a project. You'll be graded for your work as a group as well as individual work, so make sure you are sharing the work *equally*."

"Let's be partners," Marianne whispered to Christie.

"Duh," Christie whispered back.

"Your project will be to research your animal and suggest a way you can help them out. I'm going to tape a list of the endangered animals to the wall, and you can sign up for whatever animal you think best—"

There was a loud scraping of chairs and everyone crouched in their seats, ready for action.

"—make sure you walk *slowly*," Mrs. Wilson taped the list to the wall, totally unaware of the tension in her classroom.

"No running. And do not fight over animals, please. If you have problems come speak with me. Okay, you can go now."

The classroom seemed to explode as everyone leapt out of their seats and raced to the list.

"*Slowly!*" Mrs. Wilson shouted over the noise. "I said *no running!*"

"Out of the way!" Sam Snell, the class loudmouth, elbowed people out of the way. "Get out of the way. You're *in my way!*"

"No!" Christie elbowed back. "I was here first!"

Marianne had already reached the list. "I GOT IT CHRISTIE!" she shouted, pulling out a marker. "THERE ARE ELEPHANTS AND I GOT THEM!"

"CALM DOWN!" Mrs. Wilson yelled.

"THE ELEPHANTS ARE MINE!" another girl next to Marianne tried to grab the marker.

"NO WAY!" Marianne ducked under the girl's arm and slammed the marker onto the sheet, scribbling frantically. "HAHA!"

Marianne pushed her way back through the crowd to where Christie stood. "Whew. That was close," she said.

There was a weird look in Christie's eyes. "Did you say there were elephants on the list?"

"Yep! Asian elephants. And we got them!" Marianne said

proudly. Then she noticed Christie's expression. "What's the matter?"

"I can't believe elephants are endangered," Christie said. "That's—that's terrible. Can you imagine what would happen if pink elephants were endangered? Or if Pink Elephant was the only one left? He would have never found where he belonged and he would have been so sad."

Marianne bit her lip. She had been so excited about the list, she hadn't realized what it meant.

"Last time we had a project, Pink Elephant helped me make it so much more amazing than it ever could have been if I had just done it on my own," Christie said slowly. "Maybe he can help us out again."

"You're right," Marianne said, fire in her eyes. "I'm sure he'll know what to do."

That afternoon, the four friends gathered in Mandy and Christie's room. Pink Elephant sat on Mandy's shoulder, looking worried.

"Listen up," Christie said seriously. "I asked you guys to all come over because we got a problem. Elephants are endangered."

"What does that mean?" Peter wanted to know.

"It means there aren't many left," Christie said. "And some-times there are so few of them left that they can't find each other and then they can't have families. And then they eventually die out and there are none left on Earth."

Mandy felt like crying. "Elephants?"

"Imagine what would happen if there were no more elephants left in the entire world," Marianne said.

Peter shook his head. "We can't let that happen!"

"I'm hoping if we do enough research we can find out a lot about them," Christie said. "Dad always says that the more you know, the more you can change the world. Right?"

Mandy nodded. "He says that all the time."

"This might just be for a project for school, but I really want to learn more about them," Christie said.

"Let's go to the library now!" Peter said. "Mandy and I will help you guys research!"

"Yeah!" Mandy said. "We'll do the best job ever."

"If only there were some way we could actually go see the elephants," Christie sighed. "It would probably help us learn more than any book or website would."

"Like *that's* going to happen," Mandy said.

"I know," Christie said. "Mom's not exactly gonna let us fly out of the country, is she?"

Suddenly Mandy gasped. "Pink Elephant could fly us there at night," she said excitedly. "Mom would never know!"

"That's right!" Christie said. "It's perfect!"

Marianne shook her head sadly. "No guys, it's not going to work. Even flying on an airplane it takes Peter and me like, sixteen hours to get to China. Even if the second you got there you turned around and flew back you'd be missing for more than a day."

Christie slumped down on her bed, disappointed.

"Pink Elephant?" Mandy asked softly. "You've been very quiet this whole time. What are you thinking?"

"There *is* a way you could go visit the elephants," Pink Elephant said slowly. "But it's very dangerous."

"What is it?" Marianne leaned forward in her seat.

"Well," Pink Elephant said, "remember how I vanish in a pink flash of light whenever I go back to Pinky Land? I don't really actually *fly* there."

"What do you do?" Peter asked.

Pink Elephant smiled. "I think it's time I told you about the Great In-Between."

# The Great In-Between

"It's important that you understand something first," Pink Elephant said seriously. "Traveling through the Great In-Between isn't just like closing your eyes and making a wish. I found out that even through it's easy for me, for humans it is much harder."

"What do you have to do?" Peter asked.

Pink Elephant thought hard. "It's like all over the world there are doors you can't see, full of shortcuts from one place to the next. I travel through these doors to go wherever I want. It's like traveling through a tunnel."

There was a pause while everyone tried to understand this.

"A shortcut?" Mandy asked. "Like instead of walking all the way to school, you step into this short tunnel and arrive at school only a few steps later?"

"Yes," Pink Elephant said.

"Is there a door in this room now?" Peter asked.

Pink Elephant nodded. "There's a weak spot right here," he made a circular motion in the air with his trunk above Mandy's head. "You see, the doors aren't really there. I make doors out of the weak spots. I also control where the other end of the tunnel goes. In Pinky Land, we call the tunnel 'The Great In-Between'. In order to be able to move through the Great In-Between, you have to be in tune with your surroundings."

Peter looked at the empty space where Pink Elephant had pointed and put his hand up to it. "Is my hand in the door?" he asked.

Pink Elephant shook his head. "The door isn't there until a pink elephant makes it there. Your hand is in the weak space, but if you're not concentrating the right way you'll just walk through it."

"What?" Mandy said, totally lost.

"Pretend that it's like a piece of paper," Pink Elephant said, picking up a sheet of notebook paper from Christie's desk. "There are weak spots in it, like when paper gets dabbed with water." He used his special abilities to make the paper float in the air, then sucked up a little water from a glass on the edge of Mandy's nightstand and sprinkled water gently onto a few places on the paper. Dark, wet spots spread outward, and the paper sagged. "If I wanted to go through the paper, I would choose one of those weak spots to go through." He tapped the paper in a wet spot. The paper broke, and Marianne giggled as Pink Elephant's trunk tickled her on the other side of the paper.

"Going through the tunnel is a shortcut, like Mandy said. It takes much less time and you don't have to walk or run or drive so far. But it takes a special ability to go through. When you step into the tunnel, your body changes. Instead of looking the way you do now, you would become just energy. Like electricity. And then you turn normal again at the end of the tunnel. It's like an ice cube melting into water and then being frozen into an ice cube again. When it's melted, it's in a different form. But you can freeze it back into its regular shape later. Most humans can do it, if they're trained, but they can only travel with a pink elephant, or someone else who has the ability to make the doors and tunnels."

"Can Twonkie-Twonkie do it?" Mandy asked. "You said he flew with you all the way here from Twonkie Land."

"Twonks are much better at it than humans are, but they also need a pink elephant to go with them. They can't do it on their own." Pink Elephant explained. "If you want to go see the elephants, I will have to train you. Do you want to be trained?"

"Does it hurt?" Mandy asked.

"Of course not!" Pink Elephant said. "I do it all the time."

"Then definitely!" Marianne said, very impressed. "We're gonna be like cool sci-fi dudes that warp into other places!"

"How do we get trained?" Mandy asked.

"It will take a long time," Pink Elephant said, "but the first step is to be able to concentrate very, very well."

"I try to sit still when we go to concerts," Mandy said. "Like for Christie's band concert—I didn't move the entire time! That's concentrating, right?"

"That is very good," Pink Elephant said, "but you will have to concentrate even harder than that to do space-travel."

"Let's try now!" Peter exclaimed.

"I don't know," Pink Elephant said doubtfully. "You need to practice a lot."

"Please, Pink Elephant?" Mandy begged.

"Alright," Pink Elephant sighed. "Close your eyes, and breathe deeply. Think only about traveling. Nothing else."

The four children closed their eyes, Mandy scrunching hers tight. For a few minutes, there was nothing but the sound of breathing in the room.

Peter opened his eyes first, and then Mandy opened her eyes, and then Christie and Marianne.

"What happened?" Mandy looked around. "We didn't move!"

Pink Elephant nodded. "You're not ready yet, but I wanted to see how well you could concentrate on the first time. You are all doing very well. We will probably be able to travel in a couple weeks."

"A couple weeks!" Peter exclaimed. "Why so long?"

"It's very difficult to train," Pink Elephant said sternly. "Luckily because you spent so much time with Twonkie-Twonkie and me, you are already half-ready because you are more aware."

"Can we try again?" Mandy asked, eyes shining.

"I don't think it's a good idea," Pink Elephant said kindly. "If you do it too much at first, you'll wear yourself out. You should rest for a bit. We'll try again in the morning. But for now, let's do some research on the elephants!"

# The Great Attempt

FOR TWO WEEKS, EVERY DAY AFTER SCHOOL, PINK Elephant coached his four friends in Mandy and Christie's room. In-between hours at the library, where they tried to learn as much as they could about Asian elephants, they went back to the Evans' house and did exercises with Pink Elephant. They practiced concentrating for the first week, and in the second week they started learning how to feel for the opening of the Great In-Between tunnel that Pink Elephant would make. At the end of the second week Pink Elephant was ready to start traveling.

"Are you sure we can do this?" Mandy and Christie sat on the curb of the sidewalk outside their home as they waited for Marianne and Peter to arrive. Christie had her nose buried in an encyclopedia, and Mandy had a National Geographic book full of elephant photographs.

"I think so," Pink Elephant said. His tail was swinging from side to side, and Mandy knew he was nervous.

"What happens if we don't make it out of the tunnel?" Mandy wanted to know.

"Don't think about it," Pink Elephant said. "I don't want to distract you. But if it makes you feel better, you won't be able to even enter the tunnel until you feel ready. If you're not calm and focused, you won't be able to go into the tunnel at all. As long as you focus on your energy and the Great In-Between, everything should be fine."

Peter and Marianne rounded the corner at the end of the street, and Mandy and Christie stood up.

"Are you guys ready?" Christie said, a grim expression on her face.

"We think so," Peter said.

"Let's go to that middle school near our house," Marianne said. "It has soccer fields, and they're usually deserted on Sunday mornings."

The four friends and Pink Elephant walked slowly to the school in silence, trying not feel nervous. Marianne led them through a shortcut all the older kids used: a dry wash that was thick with shrubs. The wash passed by the school soccer fields, where there was a tall fence. The gates were unlocked, and Marianne swung them open. The fields were completely deserted, just as Marianne had said. Everyone stopped at the edge of the fields, where there was a strip of gravel, and stared at the tall, brick buildings of the middle school.

"Here goes," Mandy said. They started walking across the wet grass until they were on the opposite end of the field, facing the fence.

"Okay," Pink Elephant said. "There's a weak spot right here. Let's try this standing up. Focus on your destination. We want to go to the other end of the soccer fields. Let's aim for that bush of pink flowers over there," he pointed his trunk at a small flowering bush next to the gates leading out to the wash. "Close your eyes. Breathe deeply and feel the air around you."

Pink Elephant grew to a larger size and stood between the four children. The air in front of him sparked strangely, and then began to shimmer into strange shapes. Pink Elephant started to glow, and the shimmering air began to stretch until it was shaped like a large archway just big enough for all five to go through. Pink Elephant glowed a little brighter, and the air changed again. It was as though the air had become a thick sheet of unbreakable glass. At the far end of the field, near the flower bush, a similar arch began to form.

"Feel the Great In-Between," Pink Elephant murmured, taking a step toward the arch. Smoothly, together, as though in a trance, all four children stepped forward to match Pink

It was shaped like a large archway
just big enough for all five to go through.

Elephant. They moved as one, all moving the same foot, moving the same distance, moving at the same time.

"Concentrate," Pink Elephant reminded them. He took another step forward, until his trunk was just brushing against the opening of the archway.

He took a deep breath, and then all five of them stepped into the still archway in a flash of pink light. The archway rippled and swirled inward, and then vanished, leaving Christie and Marianne, asleep on the grass. At the other end of the field the archway shimmered and Pink Elephant, Mandy, and Peter drifted slowly out. The archway glittered, warped, and then vanished.

"Now think about where you are," Pink Elephant said. "When you feel in tune with your surroundings again, open your eyes."

Mandy and Peter opened their eyes slowly, staring at the bush in front of them.

"Oh my gosh!" Mandy screamed, "we did it!" She threw her arms around Pink Elephant.

"That's so awesome!" Peter jumped up and down. "Let's do it again!"

"Wait," Mandy said, pulling back. "Where are Marianne and Christie?"

Pink Elephant looked back, and Mandy gasped. "Christie!" She ran back across the fields and knelt next to her sister.

Christie opened her eyes slowly. "What happened?" she asked groggily. She sat up slowly. "We didn't move!"

"But *we* did!" Peter said excitedly. "Mandy and I traveled all the way over there!" He pointed to the end of the fields.

"What?" Marianne rolled over, suddenly awake. "How come we didn't travel?" she groaned and bent over. "I feel sick."

Pink Elephant touched his trunk to her forehead, and Marianne felt a warmth swell inside her.

"Thank you Pink Elephant," she said. "That feels much better."

"Did you see anything?" Christie asked.

"A lot of flashes of light," Mandy said. "It was such a short trip that there wasn't much to see."

"How come they didn't travel?" Peter asked Pink Elephant.

Pink Elephant smiled. "Don't worry. It just means they weren't in tune enough to go through the Great In-Between. It happens sometimes. You walked right through the door, without entering the tunnel. Basically it's just like you used to do—you walked through the weak spaces without noticing."

"Does this mean we'll never be able to travel?" Christie asked, troubled.

"Of course not!" Pink Elephant said, encouragingly. He held out his trunk to her and helped her to her feet. "It just means you need to try a little harder. It is very difficult. Mandy and Peter probably learned a little faster than you did because they are younger."

Marianne yawned. "I would love to try again, but I really am exhausted."

Pink Elephant nodded understandingly. "That's quite alright," he said. "It's normal to be tired after the first few times. Let's go home."

# Close Encounters of the Pink Kind

A FEW DAYS AFTER THEIR FIRST TRY ALL FOUR OF THEM were able to travel to the end of the field. They practiced this for another week, and then they tried going from the fields to another spot in the wash, and then from their homes to a mountaintop in the Rocky Mountains, and finally even onto the rooftop of a building in New York.

Of course, they did sometimes run into a bit of trouble.

The fifth time they used the Great In-Between, Christie and Marianne managed to travel, although they hadn't been concentrating hard enough. They had aimed for the middle of Central Park in New York City, but ended up at the top of a platform on the USS Alexander, a navy ship that had been turned into a museum in the middle of the Hudson River.

"Something's wrong," Marianne complained, keeping her eyes shut. "It doesn't feel like a park to me."

Mandy opened her eyes. "Whoa!"

"We are in the forward main battery control tower of a navy battleship!" Pink Elephant said excitedly, looking down. No one asked him how he knew these things. Everyone was used to it by now. He did, after all, read a lot.

"Cool!" Peter said.

"Hey!" someone shouted. "Hey! Kids! What are you doing up there?"

"Uh-oh," Mandy said.

"You're not supposed to be up there! Didn't you read the sign?" the security guard started climbing up towards them, using the metal handles that stuck out from the side of the tower.

"Quick, do something!" Marianne panicked. "Let's get outta here!"

"We can't just vanish in front of him!" Peter protested. "We have to keep Pink Elephant a secret!"

"It doesn't matter," Christie hissed. "They won't know who we are once we disappear! Use the Great In-Between! C'mon, guys..."

"It's not working!" Peter tried harder. "I can't concentrate when it's this stressful!"

"It's not working!" Peter tried harder.

By now the man had almost reached them. Pink Elephant quickly shrunk to his keychain size and hid in Mandy's pocket.

"Hey!" the man climbed onto the platform. "What do you kids think you're doing?"

"Um, we're sorry?" Marianne said.

"Where are your parents?"

"Uh, they're not here, uh, right now," Christie said. "We, uh, went out without them."

The security guard frowned. "I'm calling the police," he said. "They're gonna drive you straight home!"

Mandy giggled nervously. How could they tell the guard they lived in *California?*

"It's gonna be a lo-ong drive," Peter said under his breath.

"What did you say?"

"Nothing," Peter said.

"Go on down," the guard pointed at the ladder and then at Peter. "You first. Make any sudden moves and I'm calling the police. Pesky little kids."

"Don't do it!" Marianne said in a deep voice. "We're not kids. We're—aliens, come to visit your planet."

"Yeah right," the guard rolled his eyes.

"He is serious," Peter joined in.

"'He?'" The guard stared.

"Can't you see?" Peter pointed at Marianne. "He is clearly a male alien."

"Okay, enough of this. Get down, now."

"If you upset us, we will have to call for our spaceship," Christie said. "You cannot catch us. We will fly away on our Pink Elephant device."

"Kids, I'm loosing patience—"

Mandy pulled out Pink Elephant. "I guess I have no choice."

The guard stared at what looked like a pink elephant keychain. Then he started laughing hysterically.

"That's a good one," he said, wiping tears from his eyes.

Peter looked at his friends. "I think it is time we return to the Great In-Between," he said.

"Yes," Marianne nodded. "Activate the Pink Elephant device."

Trying hard not to laugh, Pink Elephant began to grow bigger and bigger. The guard stared, then started screaming in a high-pitched voice.

"Silence!" Peter said. "Or else we will have to take you with us!"

The guard shut up, shaking a little bit.

Once Pink Elephant was the right size, the four children hopped on.

"Farewell, Earthling," Peter said. "If you speak of this to anyone, we *will* meet again."

The guard watched in awe as Pink Elephant took off, flying higher and higher into the sky. Soon, they were nothing more than a pink speck among the clouds.

As they practiced more and more, everyone noticed they could pay more attention to what was going on around them. Traveling through the Great In-Between was easier and easier, and they didn't end up in strange places as much anymore.

There were a few times, though, when even *they* got distracted.

It happened when they were in school, while Christie and Marianne's class were using class time to do more project research.

"Go to the World News Now website and see if anything new has happened with your animal," Mrs. Wilson said.

For a moment there was nothing but the sound of typing. Then someone started screaming.

"Oh my gosh!" Sam Snell shouted. "Look at the front page!"

"What? What happened?"

Everyone gathered around Sam's computer.

"Oh c'mon, Sam," Christie rolled her eyes. She and Marianne were the only ones who hadn't moved from their seats. "Don't be such a drama queen."

"Shut up! This is important!" Sam clicked on a link. "Aliens are here!"

"*What?*" Now even Christie had to get up. "What are you talking about?

"'Aliens were spotted last weekend in New York,'" Sam read aloud. "'People claim to have seen giant pink flying spaceship. Guard claims four aliens visited the USS Alexander.' Look! There are comments by this astronaut guy, and the editor of *Hoax* magazine. The astronaut guy says it's true...but the magazine dude says it's totally false."

Marianne rolled her eyes. "Who is this guy?" she whispered to Christie. "What does *he* know?"

Christie crossed her arms.

"Oh my gosh," one girl started freaking out, "it's true. What my dad has been saying is true. There really are aliens!"

"No way," another girl said. "Didn't you hear the guy? It's clearly fake!"

Marianne and Christie sighed as the class got into an argument. It was going to be a long day.

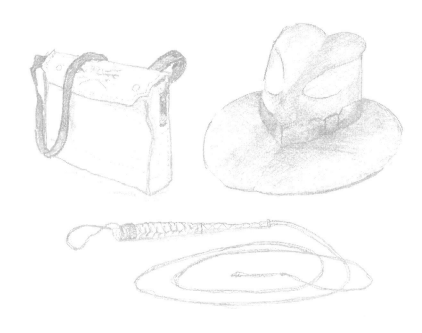

# Mission Impossible

There was never a dull moment when Pink Elephant was around. Between their schoolwork, the endangered species project, and practicing with the Great In-Between, there wasn't a lot of time for anything else. All they had to do now was decide where they were going to go.

Marianne's research showed that Asian elephants lived mostly in places like India and Thailand. For a while they had planned on going to India, until Christie suggested they go to one of the places where there were fewer elephants.

"We want to stop elephants from being wiped out," Christie explained. "We want to go somewhere where there aren't a lot of them. They need our help more than elephants in India and Thailand do."

Pink Elephant looked up from a giant map. "How about Laos?" he asked.

Everyone stared down at the map. Laos looked kind of

like a stick of broccoli to Mandy. It was right under China, in-between Thailand and Vietnam. Mandy had never heard of Laos before. She wondered what it was like.

Mandy shivered.

"What is it, Mandy?" Peter asked.

"It's just, I've never gone to a place that far away before," Mandy said. "The farthest away I've ever been was that time we used the Great In-Between to go to New York."

"Don't worry," Pink Elephant flew onto her shoulder. "We'll be with you. If you ever go anywhere, you should always go with your friends."

Mandy nodded and, sniffing a little, picked up another

book about elephants. She was reading about poachers, people who hurt elephants so they could steal their tusks, the long, white, horn-looking things that stuck out on either side of elephants' mouths. Tusks were used to make ivory, and were worth a lot of money. Poachers sometimes laid traps for the elephants, and the traps hurt the elephants, too. Mandy kept reading, and then felt her heart stop.

It couldn't be true. It just couldn't.

She dropped the book.

"What is it?" Pink Elephant asked.

Everyone gathered around as Mandy pointed to the sentence she had just read: *Experts believe that elephants will disappear in only a hundred years.*

Christie hugged Mandy comfortingly. "A hundred years is a long time," she said.

"Sleeping Beauty slept for a hundred years," Peter tried to put in helpfully. "Remember how long that was?"

Mandy wiped tears out of her eyes. "I don't care," she hiccupped. "I want them to be here *forever*. Elephants have already been here for thousands of years! We're hurting them and taking away their homes. Elephants might be around for a while, but what if one day in the future there are no elephants? What kind of world would it be?"

Everyone fell silent. None of them could imagine a world without elephants.

"Somebody has to stop the poachers!" Mandy shouted.

"Nothing's going to stop them," Christie groaned. "I've read like a hundred times that it's impossible to catch them all."

"No! We *have* to do *something!*"

Christie felt as depressed as Mandy did. "I know what you mean, Mandy," she said. "But poachers are sneaky. And there are so many of them! It's impossible."

"Nothing is impossible!" Mandy shouted. Everything she had learned about elephants getting hurt made her really upset. "Everyone says that things are impossible, but look at us! A year ago we would have said being friends with a flying pink elephant was impossible. Christie, kids at school told you your neighborhood project was impossible. Nothing is impossible if we try!" She turned to Pink Elephant. "C'mon Pink Elephant," she pleaded. "There's got to be *something* we can do."

"Hey," Peter said. "I have an idea."

Everyone turned to look at him.

"What if we don't just visit the Asian elephants," Peter said in a hushed voice. "What if we *rescue* them too?"

"You mean—" Mandy stopped herself, swallowed, and tried again, "you mean, stop the poachers?"

"Exactly!" Peter leapt to his feet. "It'll be awesome. We'll make the best team! We can use the Great In-Between to go anywhere and find anyone!"

"But we don't know how to *find* the poachers," Marianne complained.

"We'll figure it out when we get there," Mandy said, getting excited. "C'mon, Marianne. We can at least try."

"Is it safe?"

Mandy hugged Pink Elephant tightly. "We have Pink Elephant on our side," she said. "I'm sure everything will be all right."

"Let's do it!" Peter cheered.

"Marianne? You in?" Christie looked at her friend. Marianne sighed, then looked down at the book in her lap, which was opened to a beautiful picture of an elephant drinking from a river. The sun shone cheerfully above it, and there was a baby elephant peeking out from between the mother's legs.

Slowly, a smile spread over Marianne's face. "Yeah," she said. "I'm totally in."

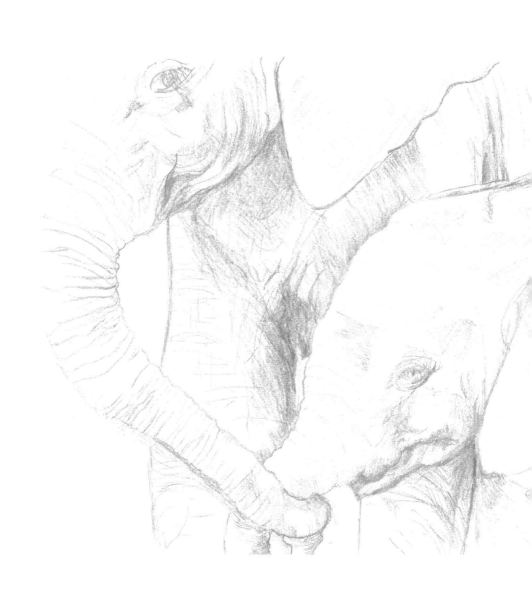

# In the Jungle, the Mighty Jungle

"THE COAST IS CLEAR, I THINK," MANDY WHISPERED, A huge pair of binoculars held up to her eyes. "It's hard to see much in the dark."

It was nighttime, and the four friends were outside Twonkie-Twonkie's cave in the forest, dressed in their hiking gear. The girls wore their Wilderness Scout camping uniforms, while Peter had on the clothes he usually wore when he and his dad went hiking together. Pink Elephant, Mandy and Christie had snuck out of the house and gone together to pick up Marianne and Peter. They had all then gone to the cave, since Twonkie-Twonkie was coming with them. Pink Elephant had gone ahead to Laos to make sure everything was safe, and then he was coming right back to get them.

Twonkie-Twonkie shuffled out of his cave. "Um, um, can Twonkie, um, eat foood first?"

"Shhh!" Mandy said. "Here, try some of this!"

She reached into her backpack and pulled out some licorice. It seemed to vanish in her hands and she gasped, staring.

"Wh-where'd it go?" Christie stammered.

"Yum," Twonkie-Twonkie said. "Um, do you have, um, any mooore?"

"You *ate* it!?" Peter said. "We didn't even see you move!"

"I guess what Pink Elephant said about twonks is true," Marianne laughed. "They really *do* move fast when they eat!"

Suddenly the bushes rustled and Twonkie's favorite squirrel rushed out, stopping right in front of them.

"Um, Twonkie is sorry, Scuarral," Twonkie-Twonkie said, "but um, you cannot, um, come along."

Mandy could have sworn she saw the squirrel sigh. A second squirrel with long eyelashes ran up next to it, and the two dashed off into Twonkie's cave.

"Who's the other squirrel, Twonkie?" Marianne asked. "I haven't seen it before."

"Her name is, um, um, Moon," Twonkie said. "Moon says, um, that she will, um, um, clean the dishes and, um, sweep the cave while Twonkie is, um, gooooone."

"You have dishes?" Christie asked.

Twonkie hung his head. "Um, nooo. Twonkie accidentally, um, ate them when, um, Pinky brouuuught them."

"Why is her name 'Moon'?" Mandy asked.

*A second squirrel with long eyelashes ran up next to it.*

Twonkie smiled. "Um, um, when she was, um, born, it was a full, um, moon," he explained.

Peter frowned. "Doesn't that mean all her brothers and sisters are called 'Moon'?"

"Well," Twonkie-Twonkie said, "she was born first, so, um, um, she does not need, um, a number. Um, her brothers and, um, sisters, are called, um, 'FiMoon,' 'SeMoon,' 'ThiMoon,' and 'FoMoon,' like, um, the, um, numbers."

"First, second, third, and fourth," Christie said excitedly. "I got it!"

"It's kind of weird, though," Peter said. "'FiMoon' is actually born second, right?"

"Um, yes," Twonkie-Twonkie said. "But, um, they never, um, get it mixed up."

"Do all squirrels do that?" Mandy wanted to know.

"Um, of course."

Scuarral reappeared in the entrance to the cave, squealing in a high-pitched voice, his small paws on his hips. He turned around and vanished inside again.

"Scuarral is, um, angry that um, Twonkie ate the dishes," Twonkie explained. "He is, um, a very clean scuarral."

Mandy snuck up to the entrance of the cave and peeked in. Moon was sweeping the floor with her tail. Scuarral accidentally got in the way and Moon started scolding him. Mandy smiled.

There was a flash of pink light and Pink Elephant appeared. "Okay," he whispered. "I think we're ready to go. There's no one on the other end of the Great In-Between."

Everyone gathered around him and put their hands on his back, closing their eyes and matching their breathing together, as they had been taught to do. Mandy was a little nervous, since they had never traveled with Twonkie-Twonkie before, but she pushed the thought away and tried to focus. A low, humming note swirled around them and they realized with surprise that the sound was coming from Twonkie-Twonkie. The note was soft and comforting, and everyone relaxed.

In front of them the archway to the Great In-Between appeared, and everyone stepped forward together. There was a bright flash of pink light, and then they were gone.

When everyone opened their eyes it was daytime, and they were in the thick heat of what looked like a jungle. Hot sunlight shone down through the leaves of the canopy over their heads. Around them the forest was a mysterious green, with soft, hot Earth under their feet. Thick weeds grew everywhere, covering the floor with tall stems and leaves.

"Wasn't it just nighttime?" Christie asked.

"It's daytime in here, since we're on the other side of the planet," Marianne explained, pulling a map out of her backpack and spreading it out. "Okay. We should be in the middle of a wildlife park. They're set up to protect the animals that live in it, but poachers come in anyway."

"It's so sad," Mandy said softly. "Laos used to be known as *Lan Xang*, Land of a Million Elephants. But now there are barely any."

Twonkie-Twonkie was singing in a low voice again, and everyone watched in fascination as a small, grey-brown bird hopped down from a tree and settled on his shoulder.

"That's an Indochinese Bushlark," Pink Elephant said softly.

The bird started warbling and Twonkie-Twonkie cocked his head, listening hard. Finally he nodded.

"Um, um, Bushlatch—"

"Bushlark," Peter said.

"Yes, um, Bushlatch—"

Mandy giggled. Twonkie was amazing at speaking to animals, but not so good at using their English names.

"—says that it will be easy to find elephants."

"Ask him about poachers," Mandy said, her heart beating faster. "Elephant poachers."

Twonkie-Twonkie started singing sweetly again, and the bird cocked its head before flying off.

"What happened?" Marianne gasped.

"He, um, um, says he has a friend who is, um, an expert," Twonkie explained. "He is, um, going to get him."

There was a rustling in the bushes and a second bush-lark peeked out, looked around quickly, and then hid in the bushes again. It popped out suddenly from behind a tree, gave everyone a suspicious glance, then vanished again. The first bird flew back onto Twonkie's shoulder.

"Um, Bushlatch's friend, um, is very nervous," Twonkie-Twonkie explained. "He does not, um, um, trust humans."

The first bushlark sighed.

Finally the second bushlark snuck out into the open, a huge leaf stuck to its beak so that its face was covered.

"Aww," Mandy said, bending down. "Here. Do you need help?" She reached for the leaf.

The second bushlark panicked, jumping back. The leaf fell off its beak and it gasped, snatched up the leaf with one of its feet, and looked around wildly, holding the leaf back in front of it. Slowly, it peered from behind its leaf. Peter thought he heard the first bird chuckle.

"Hey!" Marianne listened hard. "It's growling!"

"Birds don't growl," Peter said, eyes wide.

Everyone listened hard. The growling was getting louder. The second bushlark fainted.

"What's that?" Mandy whispered, holding tightly onto Christie.

A few yards away, the bushes rustled, and something dark flashed by.

"Oh no," Marianne grabbed Pink Elephant. "Pink Elephant, help!"

The bushes parted, and a large, orange and black shape emerged. Its strong paws were silent on the floor, pushing up deep, dark soil as it walked. Its eyes glittered bright, and the muscles under its thick fur bunched and rippled with power.

It was a tiger.

It crouched, ready to pounce, but Twonkie-Twonkie stepped up to it.

"Um, um, hello," Twonkie-Twonkie said.

The tiger froze, staring.

"Um, we are looking, um, for elephants," Twonkie-Twonkie said. He reached out and patted the tiger on the head. The tiger relaxed, and then, to everyone's surprise, sat down, purring. It opened one eye and looked at the four friends, standing behind Twonkie-Twonkie.

"I think I'm going to have a heart attack," Marianne whispered to Christie.

"They are, um, um, friends," Twonkie said.

The tiger looked at the bird on Twonkie's shoulder. The bird chirped nervously.

"Um, this butchlatch is also, um, a friend."

Finally, the tiger looked at the second bushlark, who was still on the ground.

"No," Twonkie said. "That butchlatch is a friend, um, too."
The tiger sighed.

The second bushlark opened its eyes slowly, staring at the tiger for a long time before carefully getting to its feet. The tiger seemed to laugh, moving back into the trees.

"This way," Twonkie-Twonkie said, following.

The friends pushed through the last of the trees and found themselves standing on a hillside of deep green grass. From the top of the hill they could see dirt roads winding through the green mountains, and a grey-blue mist hung over everything in the back, making it look like the sky was painted by watercolors. The mountains in the distance were covered in soft, dark greens, with strange shapes rising up like fingers and fists. Here and there were spots where the earth showed, and there was a roar of water where streams fell like white blankets over rocks. The river below them was a milky sea-green.

"Wow," Mandy gasped. "It's gorgeous!"

"It *feels* different," Christie said. "I don't know—it just doesn't feel the same way as the mountains at home."

"These mountains are older," Pink Elephant said, smiling. "As the saying goes in pinkelephantian, they have seen the sky grow wise."

Twonkie-Twonkie stopped to listen to the second bird, who was chirping again.

93

"Um, um, elephants are sometimes, um, difficult to find," Twonkie translated for them. "We might, um, have to go deep into, um, the forest. He is worried, um, um, about one of his good elephant, um friends, though. She has just had a baby and um, he wants to check on her. Is that, um, okaaaay?"

The four friends looked at one another and nodded. Taking a deep breath, they held hands as they started down the hill towards the jungle below.

# Hide and Seek

IN HALF AN HOUR, THEY HAD REACHED THE JUNGLE AND were having a little difficulty getting through it. Pink Elephant went first, with Mandy, Christie, and Marianne on his back, using his trunk to hold branches and leaves out of the way for Twonkie-Twonkie. Twonkie didn't need much help, though. A lot of the time he just pushed right through. Sometimes, he even pulled a tree or two out of the ground for a snack. The tiger was very shocked when this happened for the first time. Mandy, who always cared about all living things, made Twonkie-Twonkie promise he would make sure nothing was living in the tree before he ate it.

After Pink Elephant came the tiger, with Peter on his back. It was easier this way, since Pink Elephant had already cleared a path. Peter had climbed on after the tiger promised not to eat him, but Marianne was too afraid. The two bushlarks came

last, flying in and out of the trees, chirping at them and teasing the tiger by pecking it on the nose before flying away quickly.

"What was that?" Mandy whispered, grabbing Christie. Everyone stopped and listened hard, and the second bushlark quickly landed on Twonkie-Twonkie's head.

"Um, you are, um, making the bushlatch nervous," Twonkie-Twonkie told them. Sure enough, the bird was shivering and clutching Twonkie-Twonkie's hair nervously.

"I think I heard something," Mandy insisted. "What if we're being followed?"

Everyone looked over their shoulders, but all they could see was the jungle spread out behind them.

"Think about it," Mandy went on. "Poachers hunt tigers too. If they see the tiger here with a rare pink elephant, they'll want to catch you both!"

"The tiger seems pretty calm," Peter looked down at his new friend. "I think they would know if something dangerous is nearby, Mandy."

They slipped lower into the trees until they had landed in the middle of a deserted dirt pathway.

"Everyone stay close to me," Pink Elephant said. "Look out for traps."

"Um, um," Twonkie said, "what is um, a trap?"

"They're used for catching elephants," Mandy whispered

back. "They're buried in the ground and when elephants step on them, they get hurt."

Christie hugged Pink Elephant tightly. "Pink Elephant, what if you get hurt?"

"Don't worry," Pink Elephant said gently. "I will be alright. And I will keep you all safe."

"Um," Twonkie said, "um, is *this* um, a trap?"

Mandy whipped around. Twonkie-Twonkie had moved to the right in search of a snack, and was pointing at the ground, where a plank of wood had been uncovered. The second bush-lark screamed.

"Twonkie, did you step on it!?" Mandy panicked.

"Um, um, I think so."

"Are you hurt?" Marianne shouted.

"Not, um, really."

Twonkie-Twonkie bent down closer to look at the trap. Then, to everyone's surprise, he grabbed part of it and pulled the whole thing out of the ground. Dust flew everywhere and everyone started coughing.

Twonkie held the trap up to his mouth and took a huge bite out of it. "Hmm," he said. "It tastes, um, goood."

"Oh my gosh," Christie held a hand to her heart. "Twonkie-Twonkie!"

"Who knows *what* that trap was made of!" Peter said, eyes wide.

The second bushlark fainted. The first bushlark, perched on Mandy's head, just rolled its eyes.

Twonkie crushed the trap together in his hands and shoved everything into his mouth.

"Yumm," he said contentedly. "Can we, um, find mooore?"

"I told you twonks could eat anything," Pink Elephant smiled.

"He's not going to get poisoned, is he?" Peter wanted to know.

"No," Pink Elephant chuckled.

"That was, um, so good!" Twonkie-Twonkie said cheerfully. "It was so, um, um, crunchy!"

"Okay," Marianne said, still in shock. "I guess."

"Shh!" Mandy put a hand to her ear. "Did you hear that?"

The second bushlark quickly climbed into Twonkie-Twonkie's pocket. This time, the tiger growled low in its throat.

"Poachers!" Marianne whispered. "C'mon! We gotta find the elephants fast!"

Everyone snuck across the forest floor, pausing behind trees and peering out. They finally reached a clearing, and Christie gasped softly.

"Elephants!" she said, smiling. "Look!"

Sure enough, in the center of the clearing a mother elephant was drinking from a stream, her baby right beside her. Everyone watched as the elephant bent her head gracefully, her long trunk dipping into the water. She splashed the baby a little bit and the baby ran around, squealing happily. A few other elephants were nearby, watching the baby carefully. One or two of them patted the baby with their trunks.

"Oh my gosh," Marianne said, pulling out her camera. "They're so amazing!"

"Those other elephants must be allomothers!" Mandy said excitedly. "You know, the other female elephants that help raise the baby!"

Pink Elephant nodded. "Elephants care a lot about their herd. The mother always chooses a few allomothers to help her make sure that the baby is safe and grows up healthy. The allomothers take care of the baby as though it were their own. When a baby is first born, the entire herd watches over it and puts all of their attention into protecting it."

Even as they watched, the baby tripped and fell, and a few elephants quickly gathered around, helping the baby back up. One of them seemed to be comforting it, stroking it gently with its trunk as the baby shook its head, dizzy.

"Where are the boy elephants?" Peter asked. "Sometimes there are boys, right?"

"Over there!" Marianne pointed. In the distance, at the edge of the group, a few elephants with tusks wandered slowly. "They must not be fully grown yet, or they would have left the group to be on their own."

"Can I go meet them?" Mandy asked.

Pink Elephant shook his head and helped Mandy and Christie and Marianne down from his back. "You'd better let me and Twonkie go first," he said. "They might not trust humans. We have to tell them you are friends. Remember, elephants can be dangerous if they think their loved ones are in danger."

Carefully, Twonkie-Twonkie and Pink Elephant stepped into the clearing, moving slowly. Pink Elephant made a loud trumpeting noise, and all the elephants turned around. At first, the mother elephant tapped Pink Elephant with her trunk a few times, smelling him. The other elephants gathered around, until at last the mother made a low rumbling noise, and the baby ran up to Twonkie-Twonkie, tripping a little bit.

"Halloo," Twonkie-Twonkie said, patting the baby on the head.

Pink Elephant made some more trumpeting noises, and the other elephants turned towards the woods, looking straight at the four friends hidden in the trees.

"Oh my gosh!" Marianne said. "They're talking about us!"

"Do you think they'll like us?" Mandy was worried.

"I hope so," Peter said.

"Okay," Pink Elephant called, "the elephants are ready to meet you."

Mandy ran forward, throwing her arms around the trunk of the mother elephant. Marianne and Christie were right behind her, crouching next to the baby elephant and patting it on the head. The mother elephant trumpeted happily.

Slowly, the tiger emerged from the woods, Peter on his back. At first the mother looked a little nervous, but she eventually relaxed. The tiger sat down a few feet away and nudged Peter off gently.

"What's going on?" Peter asked Twonkie-Twonkie.

"Um, um, the tiger does not, um, want to scare the baby," Twonkie explained.

Peter had almost reached the elephants when suddenly the tiger started growling again. Everyone froze. The tiger was crouching low, turned towards the trees, its tail flicking back and forth. Three men emerged from the trees, and they didn't look friendly.

Mandy clenched her fists. The poachers had finally come.

# The Poachers

"Step away from the elephants," the first man said in accented English, "and no one gets hurt."

"What do we do?" Marianne whispered to Christie.

The elephants trumpeted in alarm as one of the men raised what looked like some kind of weapon.

"Move," the first man repeated.

"No way!" Mandy yelled, but her voice was shaking. She had never been more scared in her life. The mother elephant wrapped her trunk around her baby tightly. One of the other elephants got ready to charge.

"Stop!" Christie shouted, tears leaking down her face. "Mandy, don't do anything!" She didn't know what the poachers might do.

"I will count to five," the first man said. "One...two..."

Suddenly, they noticed Pink Elephant, hidden behind a cluster of elephants.

"What *is* that?" one of the men shouted, pointing. "It's pink!"

"That's even better!" another man shouted. "A rare elephant!"

"Stop killing the elephants," Mandy shouted bravely. "Or else!"

"Or else what?"

"Twonkie-Twonkie!" Marianne suddenly had an idea. "Those things the men are carrying are really delicious kinds of food!"

"Oh boy!" Twonkie-Twonkie seemed to vanish as he rushed over to the men, snatching the rope and tools out of their hands before they could even blink. He stuffed them all into his mouth, grinning happily. Springs and metal parts flew everywhere, landing in the grass.

"Um, Twonkie, um, looooves these!" Twonkie-Twonkie said.

"What's going on?" one of the men screamed, pointing a shaking finger at Twonkie-Twonkie. "He just *ate* our stuff!"

"*Wow,*" Peter said. "I didn't even see him move!"

"I'm going to tie you up now," Mandy said, pulling rope out of her backpack. "Don't move, or else the big man will eat you, too!"

"Or the tiger will," Peter said. The tiger seemed pretty excited by this idea.

"Hands up!" Marianne laughed. "Put 'em where we can see 'em."

The three men knelt on the ground, and Mandy and Christie quickly tied them up. Bravely, the second bushlark stuck its head out of Twonkie-Twonkie's pocket. It flew over to one of the men and rested on his head. Then it pooped. Christie wrinkled her nose.

"Promise you will never hunt elephants again!" Mandy said. "Or any other animals!"

"Yeah!" Marianne said. "Otherwise we'll come after you and eat everything you own!"

"Including your house!" Peter shouted.

The three men promised.

Pink Elephant had moved over to the mother and baby elephant and was rubbing trunks with them.

"Pink Elephant, are they okay?" Mandy wanted to know.

Pink Elephant smiled. "They are just fine," he said. "Everything is great."

Being carried by a tiger who is friends with you is a lot of fun. Being carried by a tiger who hates your guts kind of sucks. Peter, who had loved riding on the tiger's back, watched in surprise as the tiger crashed the poacher on its back into trees and bushes, and 'accidentally' made him fall into the water when they crossed a river. The other two poachers were being carried by Twonkie-Twonkie, who could lift them both with one hand and look for good rocks to eat with the other. Every time his teeth crunched down on a particularly hard rock, the poachers would start to shiver nervously.

"It's some k-kind of g-giant m-monster," one of the poachers screamed.

Twonkie looked around, surprised. "Where? Where?" he turned to Pink Elephant. "Pinky, why did you not, um, um, tell me about the monsters? I must, um, meet them for my, um, Earth Studies."

Mandy and Christie held back giggles. They were on Pink Elephant's back, while Peter and Marianne each rode one of the wild elephants. The baby had wrapped its trunk around its mother's tail and was following along behind, taking quick, tiny steps. Mandy had never seen anything so cute in her life. Occasionally the baby would run up next to Pink Elephant and, and the two of them would wrap their trunks around each other. Once in a while the mother elephant would reach out and pat it gently with her trunk.

"Elephants are such loving animals," Mandy sighed happily to Christie. "You can tell they care about each other very much."

"Yeah," Christie agreed, smiling.

A little while later the wild elephants stopped and let Peter and Marianne off their backs. The mother trumpeted loudly.

"Um, um, the elephants say, um, um, that they should not come too close to other humans. They will wait for, um, us to come back. Um, um, we should look, um, for rangers."

"What are rangers again?" Peter wanted to know.

"They're like policemen who wander around and protect the lands of the animals," Mandy explained. "They look for poachers but a lot of the time can't find them. They'll know what to do."

"How do we find rangers?" Marianne asked. "We don't know where they are and this place is huge! Plus the rangers move around all the time."

"Well," Pink Elephant smiled, "I think I have an idea."

"Flying!" Mandy guessed, her eyes sparkling. "We can look for the rangers from the sky!" She frowned. "But Pink Elephant, can you carry so many people?"

"Well," Pink Elephant said, "I can carry the four of you on my back, and carry the poachers with my trunk. Normally, an elephant my size can carry three-hundred pounds with their trunks, but even though the poachers put together will weigh more than that, I am a pink elephant so I can carry more. I can use my pinkelephantian powers to make them float, so it will be almost as if I am carrying nothing at all!"

"*Wow,*" Peter said.

"How much is three-hundred pounds?" Marianne wanted to know.

Pink Elephant thought about it for a little bit. "The four of you together are about three-hundred pounds," he said finally. "Or it's like if you went to the store and bought sixty-seven gallons of milk and had to carry all of them at the same time."

"That's *really* heavy," Mandy said. "I can barely carry one of them!"

Pink Elephant chuckled.

"Let's do it then," Christie said excitedly. She dug around in the poacher's backpacks until she found a large net. Within a few moments, they had tied the three poachers together with rope, wrapped them all into the net, and tied a loop at the top. The loop slipped over Pink Elephant's trunk, and soon the four friends were flying over Laos on Pink Elephant's back, with the poachers dangling below them. Twonkie-Twonkie had stayed behind with the tiger and the wild elephants.

"I don't see any rangers," Christie shouted over the rush of

the wind, leaning forward on Pink Elephant's back and looking down.

"Keep looking!" Marianne shouted back. She could see the poachers grabbing one another and looking down nervously. The four friends had been sure to knot the rope really tightly, but the poachers were still scared.

The two bushlarks were flying around them, sometimes soaring ahead, sometimes slowing down behind them. One of them flew up next to Mandy and winked. Mandy winked back.

"There!" Peter suddenly yelled. "I see a car parked by the side of the jungle there!"

"What if they're poachers?" Mandy was worried. "We should have brought Twonkie-Twonkie!"

"I don't think they're poachers," Pink Elephant said, raising his large ears carefully. "I can hear them talking, and they sound like they're worried about the animals."

The four friends and Pink Elephant landed on the grass, and the two birds fluttered down beside them. Pink Elephant quickly shrunk and climbed into Christie's pocket.

"Excuse me," Mandy called out. "Hello? Anyone here?"

There was a rustle in the bushes, and a short man pushed through, wearing grey-green camouflage clothes and a heavy backpack. He was followed by another man, also dressed in ranger clothing.

"Um," Christie said, "we have, um, poachers." She pointed to the poachers, who were collapsed on the ground, still tied up, and were breathing hard. One of them looked like he was about to throw up.

"Oh come on," Marianne rolled her eyes. "It wasn't *that* bad."

"Do they speak English?" Peter whispered to Mandy.

Mandy shrugged. "I dunno. I hope so."

The two rangers looked at the poachers, then back at Christie.

"You did this?" one of them finally said.

Christie hesitated for a moment. "Yes," she said. "We did this."

"How did you catch them?" he wanted to know.

Christie and Mandy shared a look. They both wished they had thought about this earlier. How were they going to explain how they had fought and trapped three grownup poachers?

"We know Karate," Mandy said, crouching down with her feet spread apart. "Hi-ya!"

Christie quickly copied. "Yi-yi-yi!" she shouted in a high-pitched voice.

Everyone watched in silence as Christie and Mandy started punching and kicking the air, jumping up and down. One of the poachers' jaws dropped as Mandy ran out of ideas and started doing cartwheels.

"Do something!" Marianne hissed to Peter. "They look silly!"

"Wait!" Peter said loudly, stepping in. "They are not showing you their true skills. We have been told to hide our abilities from outsiders. But I can see we have no choice," he turned to Marianne and bowed.

Marianne bowed back, and the two of them raised their fists. Suddenly, they jumped into action. Mandy and Christie sighed with relief as they watched. Even though their own

Suddenly, they jumped into action.

fighting had been fake, Peter and Marianne could do Karate for real.

"Thank goodness," Mandy whispered to Christie. "I was so stressed I forgot that *they* actually *know* Karate."

"We are great fighters from lands far away," Christie said to the rangers, panting a little. One of the bushlarks settled on her shoulder. "We have come to protect the elephants. And tigers."

The bushlark tapped Christie on the shoulder.

"Oh yeah, and bushlarks," Christie added. In the background, Marianne bent low and swept her foot across the ground, trying to knock Peter off balance. Peter jumped high, kicking the air as Marianne blocked the kick with her fists.

"Well," the ranger said, after he had recovered, "I guess that is wonderful news. Thank you for catching the poachers."

"It's no problem," Mandy said cheerfully. She was a little dizzy from all the cartwheels.

"Where do you live?" the ranger wanted to know. "We can take you home."

In the background, Peter and Marianne stopped. They turned to look at the poachers.

"Don't worry about it," Marianne said, gasping for breath. "We can find our way home."

"Normally you are not allowed here without permission," the ranger said.

"Oh, please don't be angry!" Mandy begged. "We didn't hurt any animals, I promise!"

"I am supposed to report any strangers on the land," the ranger said thoughtfully.

"We promise we'll help catch more poachers if you don't take us away!" Peter said. "We're very good at it and you need our help!"

"I guess, since you have helped catch the poachers, it is okay," the ranger said, thinking hard. He held out his hand. "It was nice to meet you. I won't tell anyone you were here."

The four friends shook hands with the rangers and watched as the poachers were loaded into the car.

"We must go and deal with the poachers you caught," the ranger said. "Are you sure you will be okay by yourself?"

"We'll be fine," Peter promised.

"Then, I look forward to meeting you again. Good luck," the ranger climbed into the car and started the engine. The four friends waved as the rangers drove off, leaving them behind.

"Now what?" Peter asked.

Pink Elephant poked his head out of Christie's pocket. "Now we go back to the elephants," he said. "And then we go home."

Marianne yawned. "It *has* been a long day," she agreed. "I hope we can stay awake in class tomorrow."

"It's been the *best* day, ever," Mandy said. "I wish we could do it again."

"We will!" Pink Elephant said, growing to his car size. "After all, we *did* promise the rangers we would bring back more poachers."

Peter clapped his hands excitedly. "I can't wait!"

"By the way, guys, your karate was amazing," Christie said as she climbed onto Pink Elephant's back.

"Duh," Marianne boosted herself up. "We're both brown belts."

"That's so awesome!" Mandy grinned. "I wish I knew karate!"

Peter smiled. "Maybe we can teach you later."

"Yeah! Let's do it!" Christie pumped her fist.

They took off into the blue, blue sky. The elephants were waiting.

# An Elephant Never Forgets

WHEN THE FOUR FRIENDS GOT BACK TO TWONKIE-Twonkie and the elephants, the tiger was nowhere to be seen.

"He was, um, um, hungry," Twonkie-Twonkie explained. "He said, um, he would visit us, um, um, the next time we are, um, here."

The mother elephant trumpeted softly, and nudged the baby elephant forward gently. The baby took a few steps towards Mandy, swinging its trunk from side to side shyly. It turned around to look at its mother, then took another step forward. It lifted its trunk up and then carefully put something dark and shiny into Mandy's hands. Mandy gasped and everyone crowded closer to look.

It was about the size of a large grape, rough and dark grey in some places and blue in others.

One of the elephants made a low sound, and Mandy turned to Pink Elephant.

"What did they say?" she asked.

Pink Elephant looked shocked. "This is the very rare sapphire known as the 'Elephant's Tear,'" he said quietly. "It is one of the most prized possessions of the elephants in the world. Even the other animals are not sure if it really exists. It is supposed to be only a legend. It is priceless."

"Wow," Peter said. "They're giving it to us?"

Pink Elephant nodded. "It has been passed down from elephant generation to elephant generation for hundreds of years. No human has ever owned it. It is supposed to bring you good luck, and whoever carries it will have the respect of all elephants."

"But we can't take something like this," Mandy said. "It's too important. Elephants should always keep this."

Twonkie-Twonkie shook his head. "They want you, um, um, to keep it," he said. "They only ask, um, that one day, um, when you are, um, very old, you return it to them."

Mandy's hands closed around the stone and a few tears of her own dripped down her face.

"Thank you so much," she whispered. "We'll take good care of it."

The mother elephant turned to Pink Elephant, and he cocked his head, as though listening. Mandy couldn't hear anything, but she knew that a lot of what the elephants were saying was too low for human ears to hear. Pink Elephant would be able to understand, though.

Christie was thinking the same thing. "I think Twonkie-Twonkie can hear them, too!" she whispered to Mandy. They looked at Twonkie-Twonkie, who was leaning forward, his face frowning in concentration.

"What is it, Pink Elephant?" Mandy asked.

Pink Elephant shook his head. "Now is not the time," he said gently. "I will tell you later. But for now, it is time to go home."

Everyone gave the elephants a hug.

"We'll come back and see you," Mandy promised. "And we'll stop the poachers from hurting other elephants."

She stepped back towards Pink Elephant and put her hand on his back, closing her eyes. A bright light surrounded the four friends, and then they were gone in a bright flash of light.

"Where should we put it?" Christie asked, when they were back on the street outside their home. At home, standing on the deserted sidewalk with the night all around them, it was hard to believe that they had just been to the other side of the world. It seemed like a fantastic dream. The concrete under their feet, quiet rows of houses, and the tall electric lamps were so different from the wild jungle and deep mountains.

Everyone looked down at the Elephant's Tear, proof that their adventure had really happened.

"You guys keep it," Marianne said. "After all, the adventures started when Pink Elephant landed in your pool."

"It's not like we'll never see it, anyway," Peter agreed. "We'll always come over and stuff."

Mandy carefully tucked the sapphire into her pocket.

"Well, we'd better get going," Christie said. "I'll see you at school tomorrow."

"Yeah. See ya."

Marianne and Peter started down the street, heading towards their own home. Pink Elephant helped Mandy and Christie onto his back, and soon they were climbing in through their bedroom window.

"Doesn't it feel great?" Christie said, pulling on her pajamas sleepily. "I've never felt this great in my whole life."

"It was awesome," Mandy agreed, hugging Pink Elephant tightly. "I could do this every day."

"Yeah," Christie sighed. "It's nice to know we can make a difference. Nobody deserves to be treated like those elephants. Right, Pink Elephant?"

Pink Elephant was already sound asleep. But Mandy thought his mouth had turned up into a small smile.

The next few days passed quickly. Mrs. Evans almost had a heart attack when she found mud and grass and leaves smeared all over Mandy and Christie's pajamas and bed, and she grounded them for a week.

"I can't believe this!" she shouted, waving the dirty bed sheets around. "How could this happen? Where did you go?"

"Tell the truth!" Christie hissed at Mandy.

"She'd never believe me!" Mandy hissed back.

"Last chance, girls. Where did you go?"

"Um, we had to go and save some elephants in the jungle," Mandy said in a very quiet voice.

"Don't lie to me!" Mrs. Evans kept shouting. "What were you really doing?"

Christie sighed. "We were looking for buried treasure in the backyard."

"I knew it," Mrs. Evans looked furious.

Fortunately, Pink Elephant had overheard and quickly dug a hole in the Evans' backyard to make Mandy and Christie's story look real. Unfortunately, he had gotten a little carried away and had accidentally dug up one of Mrs. Evan's favorite rosebushes.

Mrs. Evans gave Mandy and Christie trash duty and kitchen duty for another week. Mandy and Christie looked at each other and sighed. It was tough work, keeping their adventures a secret. But it was totally worth it.

Being grounded actually gave Christie more time to work on the project. Everyone else pitched in, and the four friends had fun spending time together, making the presentation the best it could be.

Part of a nail from the trap had fallen into Twonkie-Twonkie's pocket while he was eating, so Christie put it into a large glass jar to present to the class. They printed out the pictures Marianne had taken of Laos, most of which were of the elephants, the poachers, and the mountains nearby. Of course, there were a few pictures of the bushlarks. Mandy giggled as she pasted the pictures onto Christie's posterboard. The second bushlark was pretty dramatic, and was

posing like a model in some of the shots, puffing itself up to look big and bowing dramatically. Christie and Marianne typed up the story of their adventure into a report, of course leaving out the parts where they spoke to animals and were rescued by a twonk from another planet. All in all, the friends agreed that this had to be one of the *best* projects ever made. Everyone agreed that Christie would begin the presentation, and she practiced nervously for hours in front of the bathroom mirror. She wanted it to be perfect, so everyone would know how important elephants were.

"It's true, that elephants are disappearing," she rehearsed, holding a toothbrush like a microphone. "And that is something we should be worried about. But not only because elephants are some of the kindest, most loving animals I have ever known. Elephants look out for other animals. When there is no rain and rivers dry up, elephants use their strong trunks and tusks to dig deep into the soil, until they find water. Sometimes, this is the only water for miles around, and the only water other animals have. Elephants also keep plains and savannahs clear by eating small shrubs, so that there are wide spaces that many animals need. They pound out pathways into areas no one could reach otherwise. Everyone needs elephants. If elephants disappear, so will many other animals."

Mandy felt tears come to her eyes whenever she heard this

speech. But she would hold Pink Elephant close to her and remember that they could do something about it. They already had. And they would again and again.

"Girls, your report was so touching," Mrs. Wilson said, handing back their paper. "The best I've read in years. You were so creative, pretending to be rangers and writing a story. There were times where I almost forgot it was a story and really believed you had caught three poachers! And that part with the baby elephant and its mother—oh, I almost cried."

"We felt like it was real, too," Marianne said, grinning at Christie.

"I have just one question," Mrs. Wilson said. "Where on earth did you get part of a poacher's trap?"

"Uh, we got it off the internet," Christie said. "You know you can get anything from the Internet these days."

"Yeah," Marianne smiled weakly. "Thank goodness for online shopping."

"You girls are fantastic," Mrs. Wilson smiled. "You're so smart, using the internet like that." She paused and looked more closely at their poster board. "Is that bird...*bowing*?"

"No," Christie said a little too quickly.

"Bushlarks often, uh, *look* like they're bowing," Marianne said. "They do it, uh, when they feel they are in danger."

"I see," Mrs. Wilson said.

After school, the four friends met up just outside the gates. Christie and Marianne wanted to show Twonkie-Twonkie their project, so Pink Elephant helped them use the Great

In-Between to get there—after they had snuck behind some buildings, of course.

"Twonkie-Twonkie!" Christie called when they arrived. "Twonkie-Twonkie, we have something to show you!"

"Where is he?" Peter asked, putting his hands on his hips.

"He's probably watering his new Aurian flower," Pink Elephant said.

"His what?" Mandy was confused.

"His Aurian flower," Pink Elephant said. "Come on, I'll show you!"

They walked towards the entrance of the cave, where a beautiful, pale green plant was growing, its roots white and long. At the top of the plant were two golden flowers that seemed to sparkle in the sun. They were shaped like large bells, and Mandy could have sworn she saw a beautiful face peek shyly out of one of them. Twonkie-Twonkie was watering the flower lovingly, humming a little bit, and the flowers were swaying to his music.

"Wow," Peter said.

"The Aurian flower comes from Twonkie Land," Pink Elephant explained. "It's how twonks talk to others on their home planet."

"How do they do that?" Marianne asked.

"Shh," Pink Elephant said. "Just watch."

127

The flowers started twinkling, and Twonkie-Twonkie set down his watering can and put his ear gently to the top flower. To everyone's surprise, the flowers opened up a little more, and the second flower moved up slightly, until it was in front of his mouth.

"Um, yes, um, um, this is Twonkie-Twonkie," Twonkie said, speaking into the petals.

"How does it work?" Peter wanted to know.

"Aurian flowers grow pods that have two seeds in them," Pink Elephant said. "They are twin seeds. One of them gets planted at home, on Twonkie Land, and the other one gets sent with the twonk on his offworld trip. The twonk can then plant it anywhere, and the two flowers are connected no matter how far apart they are. So you can use them like a set of telephones."

"Cool," Peter said.

"The flowers are very strong," Pink Elephant went on. "You can practically pick them up and plant them anywhere and they won't get sick or die. When you need to travel, you can roll them up and put them in your pocket. They like to be sung to, which is why they like twonks so much, since twonks are always singing."

"Gee," Mandy said, "I wish I had one."

Twonkie-Twonkie leaned back from the flower, looking a little worried.

"What is it, Twonkie-Twonkie?" Mandy asked. "Is every-thing okay?"

"Um, Twonkie just, um, um, spoke with the Council of, um, Elders," Twonkie-Twonkie said. "They said that, um, Twonkie's Earth Studies, have to have, um, all living Earth creatures."

"What's wrong with that?" Peter wanted to know.

"Um, it means that, um, Twonkie has to learn to live, um, like a normal human," Twonkie-Twonkie said.

"We'll help you!" Mandy said excitedly.

"And we'll find you a place to live!" Marianne said.

"Really?" Twonkie-Twonkie beamed.

Everyone laughed, including Twonkie-Twonkie. Mandy smiled as she looked around at the circle of her best friends. It felt good to laugh together, here under the bright sun and the blue sky. There might be times when things got tricky, or they got in a little bit of trouble. But after all, that was what friends were for. Mandy knew that no matter what happened, as long as they were together, everything would always be all right. She thought of the Elephant's Tear back in her room and remembered her promise to the elephants. They still had so much to do.

"Pink Elephant!" Mandy suddenly remembered. "What was it you were going to tell us back in Laos? You said you would explain it later."

Pink Elephant hesitated for a minute. "I'm not exactly sure, myself," he said. "But they were talking about...a legend."

"A *legend?*" Peter was excited. "About what?"

"Pink elephants," Pink Elephant said, deep in thought. "They said their ancestors, their great-great-great-great grand-father elephants, had met a pink elephant before."

"But that's impossible!" Mandy said. "We would have known if pink elephants had come to Earth before!"

"Well, we never knew that Big Foot was actually a twonk," Christie said. "And we never knew 'Twinkle Twinkle Little Star' was actually a twonk song. Who knows what other things we never knew?"

"But that's not all," Pink Elephant said. "They said that their great-great-great-great grandfather elephants knew that one day humans would hunt them until elephants had almost completely disappeared. And the legend says that the pink elephant will come again, to help them. They said that elephants all over the world know this story. They have heard it since they were babies, because their parents always tell them the story at bedtime."

Everyone was silent for a long time, thinking. A pink elephant had already come to Earth? When did *that* happen? *Who* had come? And where was he now? And the part about a pink elephant returning to Earth—Mandy looked at Pink Elephant.

There were still so many mysteries.

Also look for:

The Adventures of Pink Elephant Vol. 1

Coming soon!

The Adventures of Pink Elephant Vol. 3:  Twonkie Tales

For more about Pink Elephant visit:

www.AdventuresOfPinkElephant.com

CHRISTINE AMAMIYA is a poet and a dreamer. She grew up in Arizona, and her first poem was published in 2004 in a collection of poems titled "Colours of the Heart." A 2005 Lamont Younger Poet's Prize winner and Scholastic Art and Writing Awards national gold medalist, she has also been published in Scholastic's Best Teen Writing of 2007. Three-time recipient of the Lewis Sibley Poetry Prize, she won a prestigious Silver Award for a General Writing Portfolio in the Scholastic Art and Writing Awards and has most recently been awarded the David Ecker Short Story Prize. Christine loves black and white photography, reading on rainy days, and is interested in wildlife conservation. She is a member of the World Wildlife Fund.

VISIT HER BLOG AT
HTTP://CHRISTINEAMAMIYA.WORDPRESS.COM

KAZUO MIYAGI is a retired economist. Born in Tokyo, Japan, he grew up with lots of manga. He loves children, animals, and classic music. He lives in the Southwest with his wife Lynn and two dogs, Lily and Skip.

Breinigsville, PA USA
11 December 2009
229050BV00004B/14/P

9 780979 533211